KEY WEST STORY

Also by Rick Skwiot from Antaeus Books

Death in Mexico
Hemingway First Novel Award winner.

The passionate mystery of a son's compulsive search for his father's body—a quest that draws him into an exotic Mexican underworld of sex, mysticism, drugs, and sudden violence.

Sleeping with Pancho Villa
Finalist for the Willa Cather Fiction Prize.

"A thoughtfully layered backdrop of Mexican culture... impressively crafted labyrinthine setting...Snappy and often funny dialogue."
— *Publishers Weekly*

"Life in a Mexican town...laid out beautifully...A skillfully written portrait of an entire community. Highly recommended."
— *Library Journal*

San Miguel de Allende, Mexico:
Memoir of a Sensual Quest for Spiritual Healing

An earthy, funny and self-effacing chronicle of the author's heathen days south of the border. Sexy, surreal, and darkly comic, this vivid tale paints an intimate and sympathetic portrait of Mexico and its people.

Christmas at Long Lake: A Childhood Memory

"Skwiot's vivid descriptions of the physical and emotional landscape...are poignant, entertaining, and instructional."
— *Library Journal*

"Rick Skwiot works his own magic...As usual, Skwiot's writing is sure...And his tale has a gritty, blue-collar cachet...This is good reading."
— *Kansas City Star*

All titles available in paperback and e-book editions.

KEY WEST STORY

A NOVEL

BY
RICK SKWIOT

ANTAEUS BOOKS

Copyright © 2012 by Rick Skwiot

All rights reserved under
International and Pan-American Copyright Conventions.
Published in the United States by Antaeus Books.

Key West Story
ISBN 978-0-9835705-0-9
Library of Congress Control Number: 2011933611

Book design by Amy McAdams
www.amymcadams.com

www.AntaeusBooks.com

To my friend and patron
Charlie Wolfson, a.k.a. Señor Lobo,
who gave me Key West

Contents

Preface

Imagine a literary heaven, a place where good writers gather posthumously for their due and drinks. Where a beneficent literary goddess—Calliope, perhaps—looks down with them upon us struggling mortal scribes. And where from time to time, for her own amusement and out of genuine love and pity for us, she decides to intervene and help some worthy but misguided soul.

So she sends an emissary—say, a Sam Clemens or a Sappho, a Horace or a Hemingway—to give literary guidance and moral instruction and get us back on track. Someone who helps us fight back despair, remember our calling, and put down words that seem divinely inspired. Which is exactly what happens in the following story.

While skeptical materialists would claim that an impossibility, I'd like to believe it could happen. I know some writers who claim it does in fact occur on occasion and others who count on it.

Though on its surface this novel is a tale of writers dead and alive and folks striving to become writers, it's also a story of men and women trying to find a home in this world. And because it's fiction and set largely in America, which believes in happy endings, they most all ultimately succeed.

One further note: Though some of the incidents portrayed here—in addition to the heavenly visitation—may seem fantastic, they are not, at least by Key West standards. Most everything and everyone depicted, though fictional, parallel real occurrences and real people, for better or worse.

KEY WEST STORY

PART ONE:
HEMINGWAY IN KEY WEST

Chapter One

Con knew that Florida was a right-to-carry state. What he didn't know was that along with her iPhone and iPod Cat carried a .22 automatic in her purse, as her pro bono immigration work took her into tough Miami neighborhoods where her Mexican, Haitian, and Russian clients lived. He learned about the gun the night she discovered Eva's thong under his bed.

At eight that evening they were lounging about the bedroom of his upstairs apartment across the street from the Key West library, sipping Champagne under the ceiling fan, cooling down after a couple hours of thrashing about, deciding where they might go for dinner. A scene they'd repeated over the last few months, ever since they met one night at the Hilton Pier Bar. Then apropos of nothing—from Con's perspective—she asked: "You ever think about getting married again?"

The sound of an unmuffled motor scooter came through the open window from the street below, along with the fragrance of jasmine on a warm breeze. He knocked back some Perrier-Jouët. "My lost years with Francesca left scars."

"Might be different with the right woman."

Con studied her, trying to figure out where she was coming from. Her features were pleasing enough—a slender face, strong jaw, thin nose, pale blue-gray eyes—but mutable. Every time he looked at her, she seemed like a different blonde. Not necessarily beautiful, but she projected sexuality like the Key West sun sent heat. He kissed her toe and the warm, earthy fragrance of her came to him. "Live free and die. Just the thought of marriage gives me the fantods."

"People are meant to marry."

"Maybe so," he said switching on the nightstand lamp, finding his cargo shorts on the carpet, and pulling them on. "But I'm already married—to my writing."

He said it like he meant it. And he did. He'd devoted his life to it. But these days he wondered if "shackled" might have been a better word than "married."

Then what an odd look she gave him, he thought, as if she'd never seen him before. After a moment she nodded. "You're right, Con. It's too early to be talking about our relationship."

He held his tongue. Therein lay the problem, he told himself: She thought they were having a relationship; he thought they were, well…just screwing. And providing each other some companionship. Living life. It's what people did. So he went to the kitchen to fix them a couple cocktails and upon his return to change the subject.

He got fresh mint from the fridge and dropped some leaves into two tall glasses, added lime slices and sugar, and mashed it around with a wooden spoon. In went some silver rum, ice and seltzer. The bubbles tickled the back of his hand and the good smells of lime and rum rose to him.

But when he came back from the kitchen carrying the

mojitos he'd mixed, he found Cat naked on her knees beside the bed bending to peer beneath it.

"What are you looking for?"

"The back of my earring. Has to be here somewhere."

He moved to set the drinks on the dresser beside a hardback copy of *Sirens in the Streets*, which he'd earlier inscribed to her "with lust and longing," when something in her posture alerted and froze him. She'd arched her spine as if surprised. Then she straightened to her knees holding at arm's length the red-spangled thong Eva had worn a few nights earlier.

Con felt his breath catch in his chest. Damn. He'd been trying—really trying—to save himself for Cat and duck Eva. But Eva needed a Green Card badly and saw Con as a potential means to that end. Thus she had persisted in her pursuit of him, leading him to temptation, even though he had tried to keep his distance. Something irrational—or non-rational—always happened to him when a comely woman drew near and he saw the look of entreaty in her eyes and felt her warm breath on him. A voice inside him—infinitely more compelling than cerebral good intentions—then commanded him to answer her call.

He stood at the foot of the bed muscles tensed, a mojito in either hand. The human psyche, he thought, was a dark and profound thing. Just as timber wolves urinated to mark turf, women always left things behind. Usually something laden with meaning. If not an undergarment then their house key or their great-grandmother's brooch. Perhaps not always on conscious purpose but by dictate of their inner, prehistoric brains, which—like his own, Con noted—had not evolved worth a damn, thus perpetuating the species in its general sorry state.

"There's a relic from the past," he said with an aplomb that was not in his heart. "Have to talk to my cleaning lady about being more thorough."

Cat brought the thong to her face, inhaling. Then she looked up to him. "You bastard."

Con set the drinks on the dresser. "Relax, Cat. There's an innocent explanation. My married friend Mike used the place Wednesday night when I was at tennis. Must belong to his mistress."

She rose, stepped toward him, and slapped him. First with her right then her left. Then the right again.

Ah, domestic violence, he thought. He had figured she was likely capable of it, given her passionate nature. But this brand of passion pleased him not. So he grabbed her wrists to stop her. She sunk her teeth into his forearm to break free. Then she scrambled across the bed to the other side, reached into her purse on the floor there, and withdrew the automatic.

Cat stood naked on the bed, the gun gleaming and shaking in her hand. Con backed away, stumbling over the loveseat and landing there.

"Don't do anything stupid, Cat. It's not worth it," he said, rising and sliding along the wall toward the verandah door.

But given what he'd learned from Paolo about the politically correct way Key West cops handled domestic disputes—assuming male guilt—coupled with Cat's legal wiles, maybe it would be worth it for her. Plus she seemed genuinely insane, at least temporarily, and perhaps capable of acts she might later, in calm reflection, regret.

She came toward him cutting off his retreat and muttering through clenched teeth, "I love you."

"This is love?"

"Don't mock me, you worthless shit."

"I admit I'm worthless in some ways. Certainly not worth shooting. Put the gun down, Cat. I think now's the time to discuss our relationship. Long-term expectations. Monogamy. I'm willing to negotiate."

She stood like a statue in an earthquake, rigid yet trembling. "Negotiate, my ass!" Then she moved closer, so as if to have a larger target.

Heart thumping, Con snatched her gun hand and pushed it upward. They fell twisting to the floor, Cat landing on top, her naked body warm and moist against his chest. He threw her off and scrambled on all fours to the dark verandah, knocking over flower pots there. Cat followed, the gun gripped in her fist.

On the verandah he spied his tennis racquet leaning against the wall, grabbed it, and swung, hoping to knock the gun from her hand, but missed as she leapt back. He yanked the door closed behind him. She pushed it open and lunged through, the gun still in her grasp.

Only one way out, Con saw. As he vaulted the balustrade he heard the pop of the pistol behind him. He plummeted toward the sidewalk below, grasping for the fronds of a traveler palm to break his fall.

Chapter Two

No shoes, no shirt, no problem. However, Con was the only bare-chested, barefooted customer at the open-air Schooner Wharf Bar that night—the rectangular main bar crammed with fiftyish men in white beards and safari shirts: annual Hemingway Days, which included a look-alike contest for aging gents with too much time and money on their hands. He wedged his way to the rail between a pair of them.

The bartender looked him up and down. "You seem special tonight, Con."

"I'm feeling special, Jerry. Run a tab and I'll pay you tomorrow. I've run out without my wallet." Albeit with my balls, he thought.

He ordered a double rum with Corona chaser and carried them to the rail overlooking Key West harbor. Just a breath of warm breeze on his chest as a full platinum moon hung over the shimmering water. Masts of moored sailboats reached naked into the black sky. A scent of sea, stale beer, and grilled fish came to him. He threw back half the rum, which heated him like sunshine, and gulped the beer, yeasty, bitter and clean-tasting. God, I feel good, he told himself. Every nerve ending on alert, all six senses keen, like he was writing again. The Vesuvius Effect: the nearness of death making life ever more so sweet. And near it was. He'd heard the bullet whiz past his ear.

"God, it's great to be alive!"

Con felt eyes on him and realized he'd spoken that last thought aloud. He turned to see a square, dark-haired, mustached man down the rail puffing on his pipe and studying him. Handsome, heavy jawed, wide shouldered, daiquiri in hand, he stared at Con with intense brown eyes, deep and intelligent. Finally, after some seconds of scrutiny as he puffed on his pipe, he said, "You're bleeding," bringing his hand to the side of his head.

Con reached up. His hair felt moist, cool, and sticky. He gazed at his hand, now bloodstained. The stranger slid a metal napkin-holder down the bar to him. As Con daubed away blood, hand now shaking at the thought of the near miss, the stranger said: "Someone using you for target practice?"

Con looked at him, gauging the stranger, and shook his head. "Cat pitched an ashtray at me."

"Catch you *flagrante delicto*?"

"Not quite. Found Leopard Lady's thong under the bed."

"Quite a menagerie."

Con dipped a paper napkin into the rum, brought it to his skull, and cursed as the alcohol burnt exposed nerves. A burst of laughter came from the bar behind them, and both men turned. Five overweight, white-haired Papa Hemingways were slapping each other on the back. The dark stranger glared at them.

"Gang of wastrels at it again, the exploitation underway: Look-alike contests, fishing contests, writing contests. Even a fake running of the bulls. Anything to make a buck." Then he turned back and fixed Con with a hard gaze. "Always believed it's important never to be a salesman. Be aloof to commerce even if it kills you."

"I have been and it is."

"When feeling bad, wondering why fame and finances falter, know you're doing the right thing. That the alternative is lying and deception, the phony smile, subjugation from inferiors, and nothing else to hope for. You'll survive as I did: One way or another. Preferable to the humiliating crap one's born into and escaped. Enjoy the island and your hot cats. You're ahead of the game. Problems of privilege and excess: Too many women, too much heat, too much sensitivity. But better than a shot liver, a kid getting shock treatments, and small craft warnings when you're a day out."

Who the hell was this madman, Con thought? Likely just another Key West character who'd had too much sun and rum. But then how would he know about Con's financial straits, vaunted sensitivity, and the humiliating crap he was born into? Or maybe he didn't and was just projecting onto Con aspects from his own past and inner state. Or speaking of the general fucked-up *la condition humaine*. But whatever, it was spooking him. He brought the rum-flavored napkin down to see it soaked through red.

The man sucked at his pipe and said, "You need a bandage. My boat's over here." With that he downed his daiquiri and sauntered down the boardwalk as if compelling Con to follow. Con shrugged mentally. It wasn't like he had anywhere else to go.

*

They moved along the boardwalk past The Conch Seafood Republic, a noisy joint with a reggae band playing outside by the bar. Then up a concrete dock with broad-beamed sport-fishing boats on either side. Near the end of the slips the man stepped up a plank and onto an older but trim thirty-footer, the Pilar, with outriggers held in place by bungee cords.

"Permission granted to come aboard," he said, and Con followed him onto the craft.

The stranger went below and came up from the cabin with a first-aid kit in one hand and a bottle of Havana Club in the other. Con sat on the fantail and sipped rum while the other doctored his scalp.

"You're lucky."

"How?"

"Bullet just grazed you. And no more ashtray bullshit."

"I lead a charmed life."

"You don't seem suicidal. Accident?"

Con turned to gauge him further, but the man pushed Con's chin back dead ahead while he worked on him. He knew you shouldn't trust strangers and open up to them about things that were none of their damn business. That could get folks in trouble. All the wise guys told you. But he'd found that was no way to live. He always trusted folks and as a consequence was rewarded more in sum than disappointed, even if the disappointments outnumbered the other. Besides, there was something solid about the guy that put him at ease. And he was listening. He asked his question and now was waiting to hear what Con had to say. So he figured why not give him the whole nine yards?

"It could have just gone off. She'd chased me onto the verandah and might have stumbled and squeezed the trigger accidentally. But pulling the gun and sticking it in my face was no accident."

"You run with a rough crowd."

"She carries it for her work lawyering in Miami ghettos."

"Then she knows legal shenanigans. Maybe figured she could get revenge and get away with it. Claim rape or self-defense."

"She's hardly that cold and calculating. Rather unpredictable."

"I can see that. A literal femme fatale."

"But what a piece of tail."

"Believe me: Fucking's been around a long time and always the same for participants: You feel like you just invented it. Look. Your lady friend's trying to net you the only way she can, by keeping the seas churning, keeping you swimming round the bait."

"Live bait's hard to resist. I may even love her in a way."

The stranger shook his head. "Your generation's undisciplined. Ruined everything it's touched…There. That should stem the bleeding."

Now Con could turn and manage a good look at him. Though his eyes were marked at the corners with fine sunlines, he seemed Con's age.

"You mean 'our' generation. Another lost one," Con said, "though this time in drugs, hedonism, and intellectual laziness. Brought to its pinnacle here in the Conch Republic, sloth and chemical-addling capital of the Western Hemisphere."

He looked at Con as if studying a knotty math problem. "Too many words. Too facile. And the cynicism: Doesn't hang well on you."

Con started to argue but checked it. The words stung, telling him they'd hit exposed nerves. Also, there was something paternal about the guy that deterred outright contention. So instead of arguing, Con changed the subject:

"Wonder if she's waiting in ambush for me back home."

"Sleep down below if you want. I bunk on deck and am up at dawn."

"Thanks. She'll likely have cooled by morning."

"Likely."

After another rum Con headed below, pausing in the

gangway. "Thanks for the hospitality. My name's Con."

The man sat with his feet on the rail, lighting his pipe. "Nick," he said. "You'll find a shirt in the dresser, Conman."

Below, the cabin betrayed the boat's age: Teak with a patina of wear, brass fittings, spare. Everything neat and stowed. Above the narrow bed on the left, Con noticed a row of books: Faulkner, Fitzgerald, Dos Passos; Cather, Turgenev, Hemingway. He pulled out *To Have and Have Not*, which he'd not read for years, long before he came to Key West.

With it he slid into the bunk, flipped on a brass lamp there, and studied the yellowed, musty-smelling dust jacket. When he turned it over there he was, seemingly: Nick, the man smoking on the deck above. His resemblance to the young Ernest Hemingway pictured on the dust jacket startled Con. A nephew? Grandson? Or was it just the rum and residual adrenaline from his brush with death making him see similarities that wouldn't hold in sober daylight? Whichever, he turned to Chapter One and was suddenly in Cuba at the café with the Conch fisherman Harry Morgan.

Chapter Three

Next morning when Con climbed the gangway Nick was where he left him the night before, in the canvas deck-chair with his feet on the rail, but now with a cup of coffee instead of a glass of rum. The harbor lay silent, dew covered, and windless, the scents of sea and gasoline in the air. The sky had brightened and Con could see the sun reflecting off the top floor of the hotel to the west. As he approached, Nick nodded toward a thermos and cup on the fantail. Con helped himself.

When Nick saw that he was carrying *To Have and Have Not*, he said: "Take that with you."

"Thanks. Read most of it last night. The characters are just like Conchs I know. Still bitching about carpetbaggers raping Key West, how the cops harass folks, how good things used to be."

Nick stared off into the mid-distance. "Things were better back then. Too many people on the island nowadays. But Key West is Key West and always has been. Even in the old days it wasn't unusual to send a young man home in a box to mother because he couldn't handle the freedom. Amazing how much punishment the human vessel can take, but there's a limit. Suicide's a useful tool when deliberate and planned, but the slow kind is the helpless fool's way out."

"I'll keep that in mind."

"You're young, Conman, with work to do. You need to stay in shape and not get sidetracked. As long as pure spirit means nothing—and it don't mean much while we're on Earth—we need our mortal animal to get around."

"Would you tell that to Cat?"

"Think she's still waiting?"

"Too bad she's homicidally jealous. Otherwise she's near perfect."

Nick rose shaking his head. "You're incorrigible, Conman."

He went below and returned with a snub-nosed revolver. "You know how to use this?"

"Aim and pull the trigger?"

"Tell you what: I'll walk you over in case she's lying in ambush. A lawyer's less likely to plug you with witnesses."

*

They moved up Elizabeth Street from the harbor, the morning sun now hanging over the rooftops and warming them. Scooters, trucks, and cars whizzed past. When his place came into view, Con paused then approached slowly, for he saw something lying on the downstairs porch and feared for an irrational moment that it might be Cat. But soon he saw it was just a plastic trash bag in front of his downstairs door. He stepped through the gate and onto the porch. Bending to peer inside the sack he spied a mound of printed paper torn into shreds and, there, in the pile, the cover of *Sirens in the Streets*.

"My novel. Ripped it into little pieces. Page by page." Con stared at the cover, shaking his head. "She's still pissed."

"Apparently." Nick took the mutilated cover from him

and studied it. "'By Con Martens'...Martens—ain't that a weasel?"

"American pine martens, *Martes americana*, remarkably graceful and solitary members of the weasel family."

"Used to shoot them in Michigan."

"Open season in Key West too."

Nick nodded gazing at the shredded novel. "This is like Hadley losing the suitcase of manuscripts at the Gare de Lyon: an act of infidelity and attempt at castration. Though pretty feeble in this case. But I do have one critical piece of advice, you solitary weasel."

"What's that?"

"Never close your eyes when there's someone in the room. That goes doubly with Wild Cat. Unlike Dog, Man cannot sleep with one eye open, and eventually you'll doze off. That's when she'll unman you with her pinking shears or whatever's handy."

Con looked up toward the verandah overhead. "She probably went back to Miami."

Nick patted the pants pocket where he put the pistol. "Better make sure."

Con and Nick crept up the stairs but found the apartment empty. Nick relaxed on the verandah while Con went to the kitchen to make coffee. When he returned, Nick was leafing through *The Writer's Chronicle*, which Con had left lying on the rattan coffee table where Nick's pistol now rested.

"What's this rag?"

"From a writers association I belonged to."

"Writers association? Ha! Looks like something for schoolteachers."

"It is. After my book hit the bestseller list—alas, briefly—the writer-in-residence offers started coming in. I figured if they were going to pay me to spank coeds, why not? But my gig was aborted."

"How ?"

"Drummed out for heresy."

"Which?"

"For suggesting to my students that talent was a gift no amount of graduate school and ambition could summon. My elitism was chastised in a departmental meeting and I was duly sacked. Funny coming from a rigid hierarchy."

"You should thank them, Conman. Teaching's not for a writer. Instead of reading good, technically instructive literature, you end up reading first drafts, and all first drafts are shit. A writer should write."

"Not always easy."

"Hardest sedentary work there is."

"Tell me about it. My publisher's waiting for a follow-up novel."

"How goes?"

Con gazed up at the cloudless sky. "Maybe it's Key West. The weather's too good, the water's too warm and inviting. Plus the party never ends. A writer needs isolation, boredom, and a pissy climate to get anything accomplished. Look at the Russians."

"Others have written here."

"I'm special."

"Then go back to the shitty climate you came from or move to Siberia. Worked for Dostoevsky."

"Financially difficult just now. And life here in paradise is hard to give up."

Nick stared off, as if going into himself. "It may be paradise, but being a writer who ain't writing is hell."

"What do you know about it?"

Nick set his formidable jaw and exhaled through his nostrils, studying Con. "We're all writers, Conman, limning a faint sketch across the surface of the earth. Some of us will write books that end up in libraries for a few years before they rot or burn. But if you can write a story that's true and honest without bullshitting yourself or anyone else, maybe that's worth something fleeting. And if it's good enough it will last as long as there are human beings. Hold to The Code, Conman. It always worked for me, and when I lost the ethic my work suffered."

"What work?"

He looked at Con hard. Then he leaned forward and reached toward the rattan table. Con tensed, thinking for an instant that he was going for the gun. But instead Nick grasped the copy of *To Have and Have Not*. He turned it over and nodded toward the photo of Hemingway on the dust jacket. "You see?"

"Yeah. You resemble him."

"Good reason for that."

"Related?"

"Not exactly."

"Then what?"

Nick lifted his chin toward the book jacket and jerked a thumb at his chest.

Con studied him then smiled. "You're saying that you're Ernest Hemingway?"

"I know it sounds crazy."

"To say the least."

"I don't know how it happened. I'm supposed to be dead fifty years. But here I am." He dumped two spoons of sugar in his coffee and stirred. "I understand you're dubious. But don't dismiss me too quickly. Writers need friends, Conman. Ironic, what with people everywhere, how hard it is to get a friend."

Con became conscious of birdsong in the sand tree shading them.

Nick sipped from his cup then went on: "I think we can help each other. But we can't double-cross. Like comrades-in-arms: I cover your back, you cover mine."

Con's gaze moved from Nick to the gun on the table.

Now Nick smiled.

"No, I'm not mad, Conman, and I won't shoot you. I had my day. Now I'm like some writers who are born only to help another writer to write one sentence."

Con took in a breath and studied him, thinking, conversely, that Nick was perfectly fried. Or playing some game and it was likely best to play along. But he had to admit that Nick was the image of the dark-haired, 40-year-old Hemingway who had sat for the dust-jacket photo.

A musical *zee zee zee zee zwee* drew Con's eyes to the sand tree above. There sat a migratory American redstart, black with brilliant orange splashes.

Nick's gaze followed his to the bird. "I've been touched much by superstition and am always on the lookout for bad signs: the hex, the bastid who'll jinx you. But I've been alert to good signs too and had access to a certain type of miracle. The fact that I'm here is certainly a miracle. We need to get you one, Conman."

Con nodded agreement. Yes, that's what I need, he thought. A fucking miracle.

Chapter Four

When Con checked his cell phone next morning he saw that Cat had left a message: "It was an accident, Con. I didn't think it was loaded. Then I stumbled and the darn thing went off. But when I think of that red thong, I wish I had shot you. Though you wouldn't understand."

She was right about that. As much as he loved women and enjoyed their company, he couldn't grasp what went on inside. That's where they seemed focused—on internal, forward-looking abstractions like relationship and fidelity—not on the moment and the great pleasures that the real world offered up.

He also found a message from his best-paying writing student, Sandra: She and Paolo were setting off for Havana on her boat. Great news for Paolo, who needed some good luck for a change. But Con had been counting on picking up some cash from her at their weekly session.

So instead Con decided to see if Nick was still keen on deep-sea fishing, which he had suggested the previous day. "Maybe give you something to write about," he had said as he departed.

Con grabbed Nick's first edition of To *Have and Have Not* and, as an afterthought, a copy of *Sirens in the Streets*.

*

When he got to the Pilar he found a barefoot Filipino rigging ballyhoo on the fantail and Nick in his deckchair drinking coffee and reading that morning's *Key West Citizen*. Con noticed that Nick dressed even more slovenly than he himself did in his cargoes, flip-flops, and tee shirt with sleeves and shirttail hacked off. Nick wore a khaki shirt with epaulets, stained reddish-brown by fish-blood smeared across the front and long sleeves rolled to the elbows; baggy, white, pants—secured at the waist by a hank of anchor line—that barely reached his ankles; and well-worn huaraches on tanned feet. Atop his head sat a beige, long-billed fishing cap, it too stained and frayed.

"Permission to come aboard, Conman. Reports say sailfish are running in the Gulf Stream."

"Brought back your book and a copy of mine."

"At least you were alive to edit it," Nick said, shaking his head at the newspaper and turning to an inside page.

Con scanned the front page and saw what he was talking about: the publication of a "new" Hemingway novel. Nick went on:

"If I'd wanted it published I would have done so myself. The novel was crippled at birth and destined never to walk. My descendents have no shame. I know nothing worse for a writer than for his early writing, which has been rewritten and altered, to be published without permission as his own. I would no more do a thing like that to you than I would cheat a man at cards or rifle his desk or wastebasket or read his personal letters. Burn it all before you go, Conman. Make a big pyre and throw yourself on top before they have a chance."

Con lowered himself into a deck chair studying Nick. Yeah, he looked like him more or less, but Con was unable to suspend disbelief and swallow his Hemingway persona. But instead of challenging Nick, he let it pass, and simply said: "That would cure the hangover."

"Look at this: Twenty thousand dead in an Indian cyclone and it's on page three. Though the passing of any Kennedy or British royal is headline news for weeks. How many dead Hindus would the world trade for one princess? Didn't they ever hear of the Enlightenment, the French Revolution, Marx and Engels? Corruption's so prevalent it's considered normal. You either know this or you're part of the problem. That's why I drink: I've got a Greyhound-bus engine in a Model-A-Ford chassis. The strain. Of holding back."

"Most drunks don't have that excuse. But maybe modern existence is bearable only with painkiller."

"Back again to la condition humaine. French invention, naturally. But don't look at me, ladies. I had nothing to do with this mess." Nick tossed down the newspaper. "Need a beer?"

Con nodded and Nick had the Filipino, Bustamante, fetch him one from the ice chest.

"Where'd you get your hangover, Conman?"

"Lavish dinner party up in Key Haven at my dive buddy Johannsen's. Lots of vodka and leggy Russian dancers."

"To have fun you've got to hang with real artists, real rednecks, or the real rich—the only ones who don't give a damn. The cautious crowd can kayo a writer who lets his left drop. Just keep your head down and don't listen to nobody. The years when you're struggling are the best."

"Even if the struggle bears no fruit?"

"I wouldn't know personally, but I'd say so."

"I'm not so sure. Say there's a man wandering sun-blind in the desert. Finally by dint of marching without stop and despite the burning sun, frigid nights, and total darkness, he comes upon an oasis with date palms, cool water, harem girls, and tented orgies. Now there's a tale we might be interested in. But without the oasis at the end, it doesn't make for much of a story, does it?"

"No, but you have to live believing in the oasis. Otherwise you'd never move."

Con took a pull at his beer. "I've got to keep moving. Writing's all I ever wanted to do."

*

Soon they were underway, Bustamante at the helm, Nick and Con standing astern eyeing eighty-foot cruisers and fifty-foot yachts moored in Key West Bight. They slid by fashionable hotels with shore-side restaurants, tiki bars, swimming pools, and five-hundred-dollar Gulfside rooms. Past expensive condos with sunset views and, to the starboard, Sunset Key, where sat million-dollar homes protected by the sea.

"Fucking money. It's worth something, Nick."

"Money's at the top of the list of things that can harm a writer, along with politics, women, drink, and ambition. And the lack of money, politics, drink, and ambition."

"Profound."

"But you're right, Conman. Money has value for a writer. For above all he must be intelligent and survive as a writer. The hardest thing, because time is so short, is for him to survive and get his work done."

Con snorted. "Tell me about it. Took me thirty-odd years living in the most materialistic land in the history of the planet to figure this out: Money can get you things you want—the leisure to write, adventure, women, wine, et cetera, et cetera."

"I understand," said Nick, eyeing a new forty-foot sport-fishing boat docked at the Hilton. "I was the same way till I got some. Figured I was fine without."

"Ditto. For years I avoided its taint. Lived hand-to-mouth, frugal and free. Coming from working-class folks, I associated money with travail not pleasure, except for what you won at the track. But then my book got hot, checks started coming in the mail, and I saw that money was good. Not the root of all evil but the spring of all pleasure."

"Aye, most pleasures. Scorn for wealth is at bottom a desire to avenge yourself against Fate by despising the very thing she's denied you. A strategic way to avoid the humiliations of poverty and gain moral status. Still, money can be overrated, Conman. What did you do with yours?"

"Plowed through it like a snow-blower in fresh powder. Skiing the Alps, sailing the Med, surfing in Hawaii, Mexico, and Puerto Rico. Great wine and 'lively' women, as Steinbeck would say. But then the checks stopped before I could."

"Big checks?"

"They added up. Tantamount to a thousand trifectas. Maybe a million, give or take, with Uncle Sam doing the taking. Plus friends needed help. Strangers too. You would have thought my generosity had built some good financial karma." Con looked up to the blue sky. "But clouds lurk."

"Such as?"

He told Nick of back rent, overdue utilities, and the exodus of paying writing students—Cat and Sandra—over the last forty-eight hours. "But something will turn up soon and I'll get back to doing my best work."

"That's what Scottie always thought, that he could write another Gatsby. And like you he treated royalties as income not capital. Got anything saved, Micawber?"

"Nada. Before I escaped St. Louis I was getting ten calls a day from collection agencies. But most of the folks they hire to dun you are deadbeats themselves. I'd ask if they ever got behind on credit cards, then sit tight and listen. They'd start pouring out sob stories about car wrecks, drug-addicted sisters, space-heater fires, and whatever other fuckups or acts of fate had jiggered them."

"Always a good knack for a writer: the ability to keep his mouth shut and listen. That's what dries a writer up, not listening. That's where it all comes from: seeing, listening."

Con sipped at his beer and went on: "But it wasn't just bill collectors that drove me away. The state was fixing to yank my driver's license for a dubious DWI. I had good tags on the wagon and was driving great but got stopped at a random roadblock. I figured the best thing to do before heading to court and losing my license was drive to Key West, where I knew I could get by with a bicycle, Birkenstocks, and bullshit."

"What have you been living on?"

"The twenty thousand I got for the Land Rover, some nice exactas at Gulfstream Park, and unemployment checks that have since run out. Kept me going while I fished for writing students."

Nick shook his head. "Now that nobody believes in the afterlife, everyone's a writer. Any of them doing anything worthwhile?"

Con shrugged. "They're writing what they know. Cat's scribbling about immigrants and Sandra's telling about all the politicians, ballplayers, and celebrities she's screwed."

"I assume I'm not among them."

"No, but you do show up in Rebecca Hemingway's book. One of your distant kin explaining how the Hemingway mystique fucked up her life."

"Jesus save us."

"Marta's writing a true-crime tome about a woman tourist who ended up dead in a dumpster behind Sloppy Joe's, a story she covered for *The Key West Citizen*. I just hope the booze doesn't finish her before she finishes the book."

"Keys Disease locals call it. The inertia and chemical addling that infect folks planted on a three-mile-long island where the sun most always shines and the rum always flows."

Con stared off at the blue horizon. "Yes, a peaceful lifestyle. Until I met Cat."

"Too small an island for a man to have too many women."

"Johannsen says that there are bad problems, like lung cancer or heroin addiction, and good problems, like having too many women."

"If her aim had been better you'd have no problems at all."

"Another bestseller would achieve the same result."

Nick looked Con up and down. "Better to write as well as you can with no eye on any market or any thought of what the stuff will bring, or even if it can ever be published, than to fall into the money-making trap. When writers make some and increase their standard of living, they are caught. Then they have to write to keep up their establishments, their wives and so on, and they write slop. It is not slop on purpose but because it is hurried. Because they write when there is nothing to say or no water in the well. Because they are ambitious. Then, once they have betrayed themselves, they justify it and you get more slop...Just follow The Code, Conman. Remember, there are no pockets in a shroud."

"Thanks for the reminder."

"But maybe you did the right thing catapulting your cash."

"How so?"

"Purification rites."

Con sensed the boat vibrating beneath him and he looked away. It was as if a curtain had gone up, and he saw for the first time the truth behind his profligate behavior. He had known in his heart but had not acknowledged to himself that his gains had been ill-gotten, a result of subterfuge and corruption, not talent and inspiration. And that if he were ever to be capable of creating something fine and true, the tainted money had to be jettisoned so he could right himself.

*

They left the island behind and headed toward the Sand Key lighthouse. At the helm Bustamante stood barefoot with legs spread. The inboard motor vibrated the deck, which bucked as they plowed through benign one-foot seas inside the reef. Con could see the approaching line where, just beyond the reef, the turquoise water ended and the deep blue began, where the twenty-foot bottom dropped off to four hundred feet and the Gulf Stream flowed.

Once in the Gulf Stream the waves built to three feet. Nick and Con took them with knees bent, grasping the aluminum frame of the canvas bimini to steady themselves. Con spied ballyhoo dancing across the water on their tailfins. On the portside a dolphin came to escort them for a minute then disappeared into the deep. Key West dropped out of sight behind them. Now whatever problems Con had back on shore washed from consciousness. All that remained were the unfettered waters and the warming sun.

"Always reminds me why men go to sea."

"The journey and the prospect of homecoming are everything, Conman. Go ask Homer."

Nick said that last bit about Homer not, seemingly, as mere rhetorical ploy but as literal instruction, and Con got the crazy idea that maybe Nick was Hemingway, a ghost Hemingway, with writerly contacts in the spirit world. Despite the ninety-degree weather Con felt himself shiver. Perhaps, like Twain's Connecticut Yankee, his head injury had transported him to a different time and place. Or worse, maybe he was dead or damn near, like Bierce's hanged soldier imagining his protracted escape in the instant between his fall and the rope snapping his neck. Maybe, Con thought, I'm still hanging in midair after my leap off the verandah with Cat's bullet halfway through my brain.

Bustamante cut the engine and joined them aft. They got to work baiting the lines, getting them in the water, and fixing the outriggers—one kind of work Con was happy to do, and he dove into it with gusto. Soon they were trolling through royal, three-foot swells that rocked the boat as they putted along. The sun hung off the stern halfway up a clear sky. Ahead to the west he could see the Marquesas lying flat and green. Nick tipped back his fishing cap and slapped Bustamante on the back.

"Every time we're out here on the blue sea under a warm sun with the smell of saltwater I think of all the hard work and suffering in the world. The poor fuckers tanning hides in Patagonia, filleting anchovies in Morocco, or crunching numbers in New York. This is how to live."

Bustamante pulled off his tee shirt, went to the cooler bungeed to the fantail, and withdrew three beers. "You got it right, partner. We lucky." He handed Con a beer and knocked his bottle against it and Nick's.

"Damn lucky," said Nick. "¡Salud!"

However, they were not so lucky at angling for sailfish despite the good omen of the dolphin. Con did catch a bonito, which, as the name suggested, was a lovely fish, like a tuna with an aquamarine racing stripe. He let it slide back into the water, a fathomless blue, and imagined a woman with eyes that color. After a few hours Nick said:

"Boosty, since the sailfish ain't running let's go further in and get some snapper for dinner."

They took up the lines, and Bustamante headed the boat back toward Key West.

Once inside the reef in clear fifteen-foot water, Con dropped anchor at Boosty's instruction and pulled out lighter gear for bottom fishing. Soon they were hauling in grunts, snapper, and grouper. Within a half hour they had a week's worth of dinners, and Bustamante began cleaning them on the fantail. Con joined in the slaughter.

"Reminds me of childhood fishing trips to the Ozarks with my dad," he said. "The gutting always thrilled me."

Nick watched as Bustamante stunned another snapper with his knife handle and filleted it. "Reminds me of a field trip to a meat-packing plant in Chicago when I was a schoolboy and a chunky guy dropping a sledgehammer on the heads of the unfortunate inmates, followed by a free meal in the company cafeteria of very fresh roast beef."

With the fish cleaning done they all stripped naked, donned snorkel masks, and dove into the shimmering blue water. On the bottom Con found a rusty anchor and chain, and surfaced to tell Nick.

"Might come in handy," Nick said and sent him back down with a line so they could haul it up.

*

Soon they headed back in. As the Pilar once again passed the moored yachts and pricey fishing-boats in Key West Harbor, Con said: "Nice to have some real money again."

Nick squinted at him. "Money ain't your problem, Conman. Problem is you're a writer who ain't writing. The one who is doing his work is not the one poverty bothers."

Con re-tied the bowline at his feet. "I'm just in a fallow period."

"How long has this 'fallow period' lasted?"

"Well, since *Sirens in the Streets*."

"How long?"

"Four years."

"You're not fallow, Conman, you're blocked. That's what you've got, you fornicator: writer's block."

"Better than a writer with fornicator's block."

"You can make light of it, but better men and women than we have died of it. The one good thing I always had to guard against it was this: Whenever I sensed it was time to begin a story I'd been mulling, as soon as I sat down at the café table with pen and paper or stood at the typewriter and knocked out a few hundred words, the whole scope and shape of it would start coming to me like a ship through a fog bank. A nice and necessary skill for a writer to have, Conman, to find freighters lost in the fog. A knack partly hard-wired in our hearts and partly learned through years of working to do it right and steer her through that narrow channel without benefit of radar."

"Yep, that's the way it feels: My ship's lost in the fucking fog and the rocks could sink me."

"Keep taking soundings and stay the course."

Nick fetched a couple more beers from the cooler and handed Con one. "Distill your standards more than ever, Conman, and keep moving with continued faith in yourself. Surely reward and recognition await a brave and noble soul who knows a word or two."

Con felt like a mouse had run up his spine. Brave and noble: That's what he had always shot for, but then, that once, fell short.

Nick took a long swallow of beer and eyed Con. "You speak Spanish?"

"*Suficiente mal,* though Mexican Spanish."

"You handle yourself all right on board, Conman. I might have something for you."

"Doing what?"

"A little sailoring."

"Sounds easy enough."

"And keeping your mouth shut about it."

With that Nick turned away to tend the line as they neared their slip.

Chapter Five

A restful and peaceful Independence Day for Con, at least at its start. He snorkeled off Fort Zachary Taylor State Park in balmy seas, swimming among black-and-yellow-striped sergeant majors, a school of speckled Bermuda chub, yellow-tailed snappers, blue-and-yellow grunts, gaudy green-red-blue parrotfish, and black-gold angelfish. The sun cut through the water, lighting the fish iridescent. Out near the buoys in twenty feet of water he spied an immense Goliath grouper and kicked down to it. Too many barracudas about however. Some sort of imbalance that concerned biologists, he had read, but that few Conchs worried about.

Back home he found an email from Cat, stating simply, "I miss you." He missed her as well but didn't indulge himself in thoughts of her svelte body. As much as he might have wanted her viscerally, intellectually he knew she was trouble. He had been drawn into dysfunctional relationships before, as with his ex-wife, Francesca. Con knew he was emotionally vulnerable to that sort of highly dramatic and romantic woman, and had to steel himself so as not to get entrapped once again. The wise thing to do was shunt tempting thoughts of her aside and make a clean break instead of responding to her email and beginning a dialogue that would no doubt lead to more trouble.

Later, as if in compensation for his self-discipline with Cat, Eva—whom he'd not seen since the night she left her thong under his bed and almost got him shot—dropped by with a bottle of Beaujolais and a bird for chicken *paprikas*. While the bird cooked she led Con to the bedroom to show him the new chemise she'd bought. Afterward as they lay side by side she said:

"You know, Cone, that I work illegal. That I am brought from Czecho by Polish labor contractor. When I come to Key Vest he takes one look and says, 'Eva, you can clean hotel toilets and make three hundred dollars per week or be my friend and work as barmaid, make three hundred a night.'" She drew line through Con's blonde chest hair with a magenta fingernail. "He means for me to sleep with him, that filthy Pole. But I say no way and choose door number three: work without papers."

Con shrugged. "You make good money, right?"

"Yes, but...When I was little girl we had a big house in Prague. Before the revolution. Papa worked with Red Army. When the Russians leave, we lose everything."

"Was he in the military?"

"StB...Statni Bezepecnost: State security. Then they make Havel president, a writer."

"Can't happen here."

"But I like America," she said, "because you can do what you damn well please. Not like Czecho, where everyone is a spy."

"I'll drink to that," Con said, reaching for his glass of Beaujolais on the nightstand.

"But I do not like America," she went on, "because men try to be women and women try to be little men. But you are different. More man. More serious. So I make you serious offer."

She sat up on the bed, took the glass from him and drank. Then she handed it back and clasped her hands together as though about to deliver an important speech to the Czech Parliament—although her bare white breasts with pink aureoles undermined somewhat the effect of her officious posture.

"Because I am illegal, if someone reports Eva to Immigration—zip!—back to Czech Republic and living like peasant. But now I am capitalist American and will make a deal:

"I need Green Card, you need money. So I pay you going rate: ten thousand American dollars. This I know from Jana and others from Czecho, Poland, and Russia."

Her bleach-blonde hair hung straight to her waist and her warm, womanly scent came to him. Con felt at sea, perhaps from the Beaujolais and the love-making and the surreality of the moment. "Spell it out, Eva."

"Two years we live together in marriage. No baby. No strings. I pay three thousand now, three hundred per month, and split rent et cetera. Plus hot sex and Czech cooking. What do you say? Is good offer?"

"Is great offer," he said, thinking of his back rent and dim prospects. But then he shook his head imperceptibly, thinking how far he had fallen. Two summers earlier he was drinking cava with his Spanish lover on a rented yacht at Majorca. What was now a great offer used to be chump change.

She smiled her crooked smile—a KGB or StB smile, he thought, the leer of a Commie double agent. A show of toughness that, he suspected, covered a childlike vulnerability. She was in fact living like an orphan, without home or family or even country. Or a father to protect her.

Eva leaned to him and pressed warm, moist lips to his

forehead, then righted herself. "After two years you are a free man. Promise."

*

She served dinner on the verandah as the sun set behind them. Afterward they strolled on Duval Street, where throngs of tourists wandered day and night.

Blood on the sidewalk outside the Bull & Whistle, where a woman lay, her face recently chewed by a pit bull, cops on the scene awaiting the ambulance. On a side street another woman upchucked out her car door. Further down Duval a bourgeois-looking man, eyes glazed, clung to a lamppost as if hugging a palm tree in a hurricane. Tattooed, pierced, and soiled teenagers lounged on the curb. As Con and Eva passed, one said to another:

"You see, man, it's like an island."

Eva raised her eyes to the night sky ahead, suddenly illuminated red, white and blue by Fourth of July fireworks shot from White Street Pier. "Too much freedom."

"Well spoken, comrade. After you see what people do on vacation you're glad they're locked up the other fifty weeks."

"Throw away key."

As they moved past Fat Tuesday's, Con saw Eva eyeing a group of seeming sorority sisters swilling grain-alcohol smoothies: all blonde or nearly so, all wearing silky tank tops and tight Capri pants with flip-flops. She turned to him.

"Tell me, Cone: Why do so many American women have big teats?"

"Because they can afford them."

"How much do they cost?"

"Ten thousand dollars for the two."

She laid a hand on his forearm. "Or fifteen thousand for three."

Eva turned crimson laughing at her own Slavic humor. But the ten-gee figure reminded Con of her marriage offer.

They passed a shop selling gold spoons and doubloons from the sunken Spanish galleon Atocha. Eva stopped and through the window studied the artifacts, maps, and placards vowing authenticity. "It is true sunken treasure?"

"Absolutely. Worth hundreds of millions. The fleet left Havana for Spain in September 1622 with gold bars and coins, tons of silver, and precious gems. But they ran into a hurricane two days out. The Atocha and other ships went down off the Dry Tortugas."

"Is more sunken treasure in sea?"

"Lots more."

"Then we can get maps and find gold!"

"Ain't that easy. The Spaniards searched for the Atocha seventy years before giving up. And it took Mel Fisher sixteen years, ten million dollars, and the lives of three divers including his son before he found it."

"But we need money, Cone."

"Then why not sell your treasure?"

She patted his cheek in feigned reprimand. "I do not sell my body, only pretend."

*

Soon they ducked into the Red Garter, a dark strip joint where Eva knew most of the girls. Her friend Jana, a Slovak, joined them at their table for a drink. The two women talked in Czech, with Eva hitting up Con for dollar bills to tuck into the garters of her friends dancing naked on the stage above them.

Jana turned to Con—apparently apropos of something Eva had told her—and asked him about his bestseller, his students, his life in Key West. He felt like he was on a job interview, which, given Eva's offer, perhaps he was.

He and Eva continued up Duval Street and moved into Virgilio's, where a Latin band played salsa and patrons danced. Con bought them margaritas. After a minute they left their drinks on the bar and edged onto the dance floor.

She moved well to music, he noted, as one might expect if she was in fact a stripper—about which she had been vague.

They walked home in the warm dark night, the noise and lights of Duval Street quickly dissipating as they strolled up Southard Street, the air fragrant now with jasmine. They turned onto Elizabeth Street and neared his place. As they did, a shadowy figure stepped from the adjacent alley. He saw it was Cat and stopped.

Slung over her shoulder was the purse where she carried the .22. As she moved toward them and into the glow of a streetlight, he saw that her hands were empty. She glared at Eva.

"Relax, Cat."

She looked Eva up and down. "I'm relaxed," she said, and turned to Con. "I just want to talk."

"Okay, talk."

She glanced again at Eva, bit her lip, and took in a deep, halting breath. "I told you it was an accident. Can't you forgive me?"

"You didn't accidentally point a gun at me. And it wasn't the first time you acted crazy jealous and wouldn't be the last. I'm not going to live that way."

"We were meant for each other."

She spoke the last like a lost child, and he fought an urge to embrace and forgive her. Instead he said:

"And I was meant to live carefree. Meant to do my work and not expend energy in domestic strife that pulls me off center. That's why I launched Francesca. I won't let it happen again. You're not going to change, so please leave me in peace."

She moved her jaw from side to side as if thinking. At last she said: "I'll never leave you."

With that she turned, crossed the street, and disappeared into the dark.

Chapter Six

Con lay low until the long weekend had passed and Cat had likely returned to Miami. Monday night, after vetting the block from the verandah without seeing any sign of her, he strode downstairs, plastic-cupped cocktail in hand. He strolled south on Elizabeth Street with no destination in mind. Three blocks down he came to a band of light falling across the sidewalk. Through the open doors of The Church of God of Prophecy he heard a piano strike a penetrating minor chord and stopped.

Inside he saw a congregation of some twenty folks, mostly older black women, rise with hymnals in hand. Their voices, surprisingly strong, broke the quiet night:

> I got a home in that rock, don't you see?
> I got a home in that rock, don't you see?
> Beneath the earth and sky,
> Thought I heard my Savior cry,
> I got a home in that rock, don't you see?

Home. That had always seemed a luxury for an itinerant writer. No permanent address, no living relatives And now, unless some manna dropped from heaven, his temporary home in Key West seemed threatened.

> Poor man Lazarus poor as I, don't you see?
> Poor man Lazarus poor as I, don't you see?
> Poor man Lazarus poor as I,
> But when he died he had a home on high.
> He had a home in that rock, don't you see?

Risen from the dead, poor man Lazarus. Any hope for the resurrection of poor man Con, he wondered? Not literally, after a fatal slug from Cat, but literarily speaking.

> God give Noah the rainbow sign,
> don't you see?
> God give Noah the rainbow sign,
> don't you see?
> God give Noah the rainbow sign,
> No more water but fire next time.
> You better get a home in that rock,
> don't you see?

Yes, I see, Con told himself. But under which rock?

The gray-haired preacher folded the blond wooden cover over the keys and rose to lead the congregation in the Lord's Prayer. Rather than join in, Con slipped on down the street. What the hell, he thought, we're all sinners. The God of Prophecy, if benign, forgiving, and omnipotent, would surely cut him some slack. Besides, as Job warned, better not to be a hypocrite. Truce, God of Prophecy: I won't say any half-hearted prayers and you don't give me any half-assed prophecy. I don't want to know what's coming, just make it something good.

He turned onto Olivia Street and sauntered on in his flip-flops, feeling the day's remnant heat radiating from the sidewalk on his bare legs. At the Key West cemetery, crypts stood four high in the moonlight, a sight that made him thirsty. He figured that when death finally came, the bar would close eternally. So he drained off his vodka and headed back home for another, thinking of Cat and the night they first met…

*

He had been out walking, which was what he did at night, walked. A hot May night with the poinciana blooming velvet orange, the bougainvillea magenta, the jacaranda pale purple. He ended up at the Hilton Pier Bar where he saw the tall Russian Svetlana tending bar. After getting a rum and soda from her he suggested:

"Come by my place for a drink after work, Svetlana."

"If you want a woman ask any Ukraine housemaid here. They'll sleep with you for fifty bucks."

"I won't do it for less than a hundred."

"Who knows, maybe you're worth it," she said as she polished a wine glass.

Then she moved down the bar to a group of folks who'd just come from the dining room leading a busboy with a Champagne bucket.

Con leaned back in his barstool sipping his rum and studying the night sky and the lights of a cruise ship moored at the dock. Warm night air, stars, the ferry to Sunset Key motoring past. He overheard the group with the Champagne talking about downtown Miami real estate. Three middle-aged men in dress slacks and silk shirts; two stylish, bejeweled women. He made eye contact with one of the women, a thirtyish blonde in white silk slacks and blouse, and smiled. "Here for sunken treasure?"

"Nothing that exciting: court date."

"Who'd you shoot?"—near prophecy.

"All I shot was half a day taking depositions when I could have been on the beach. Romanian family. Father a contract laborer but his kid back home needs an operation here. Had to arrange visas and work authorization for the wife."

"You won't get rich on this one."

"Pro bono. Imprisoned by Ceausescu for his politics

and escaped."

"Sounds like material for a book."

"Funny you should mention that. I happen to be working on a novel."

Not all that funny, Con thought. It seemed nearly everyone with a computer was working on a book nowadays. Though he didn't complain: great for business.

She went on: A mystery set in the Everglades about immigrant farm workers disappearing. But he was only half listening, noticing the way the silk clung to the underside of her breast, the fact that there were no dark roots to her strawberry blonde hair, and how generally lithe and supple she looked.

"How's the writing going?" he asked.

"Slowly. Wish I had more time to work on it."

He nodded. "The thing is to not waste time on dead-end writing and research that won't end up in the book. To write outward from the organic core, as Henry James called it, so it's solid and true."

"Sounds like you've done this before."

"I do it for a living."

"You're kidding."

He handed her his card:

Con Martens

Editor and Writing Coach

Key West

Author of *Sirens in the Streets*

"'Con'? Where'd you do time?"

"Constantine. After the Roman emperor."

"My."

"A compromise: Dad wanted 'Diocletian.'"

"I've heard of your book. Wasn't it a bestseller?"

"'Was' being the operative word."

"Well, Mr. Con Martens, what are your rates?" she asked, taking her business card from her purse and placing it on the bar before him.

"Lower than yours, I expect, Catherine. Except I don't do pro bono."

She pursed her lips. "Maybe I could use some instruction."

They ended up back at his place on the low bed off the upstairs verandah, the ceiling fan turning above them, sweat-drenched bodies writhing together, she biting, clawing and scratching, and, ultimately, screeching cat-like when she came. Afterward, as she lay spent beside him, he admired her body, all sinew and muscle, with smooth, ivory skin. He whispered in her ear:

"You're such a fine animal, Cat."

She smiled and purred. "Cat—no one's ever called me that."

*

…Now as he neared his place he spied a figure on the front porch swing and slowed, thinking it might be her again. But then he recognized Nick's square-jawed profile.

"Nice night for a walk," Con said as he moved through the gate.

"Thought so too. Hadn't seen you around."

"Haven't been out: Cat's stalking me."

"You need a whip and chair to tame that one."

"That sounds fun."

Nick shook his head. "Careful, Conman. Just as there is good cholesterol, I am told, and bad cholesterol, there's good testosterone and bad testosterone: the good being that which makes us defend ourselves and hunt and fish and thereby eat, the bad being that which compels us to charge panzers on horseback and get a hard-on for hussies with sharp claws. And you, Conman, thanks to a secret dollop of Slavic blood in your Dutch genes, have more than your share of the madcap latter."

"I'm a genetic victim!"

"Like a lobster in a trap."

"I can't help it any more than the lobster. Medical science has yet to find a cure for my age-old physical and spiritual disease, both chronic and chthonic."

"You're busting my balls with big words, Conman. Fix us a couple drinks and let's walk."

*

Con came back downstairs with a drink in either hand. They knocked their plastic cups together and headed off toward Duval Street.

"You see the headline in Sunday's *Citizen*?" Con asked. "'Fecal Coliform Happens.'"

"Meaning?"

"Enterococci in the waters at Fort Zach, Smathers, and Higgs Beaches. Scores of hotel reservations cancelled. A full-scale recession likely."

"That'll make it quieter. Sea was gin clear here before they built the bridges. A sleepy coaling station for ships, with great fishing, cigar factories and damn few cars. Cockfights and whorehouses the only onshore entertainment along with a few nice saloons selling Prohibition whiskey. Civilized, lush, beautiful."

Con knew that Nick, whoever he might be in reality, was jesting about knowing the island eighty years earlier, as if he had gotten unstuck in time. Except for his eccentric insistence on his Hemingway persona, he seemed eminently sane and was good company. So Con didn't want to chase him off by exposing his bluff. That's what Con told himself consciously, though another, deeper part of him—the romantic, writerly part—was swallowing the bait whole.

"The world was okay earlier," Nick said as they ambled through the warm, humid night. "Don't let no one tell you different. Even a thousand years ago people ate well and fornicated and somehow lived life."

"Great if you were a knight errant and not some slogging serf."

A motor scooter sans muffler banged past, causing Nick to pause before replying: "Which is why I left Oak Park and the Protestants soon as I could. Just a hundred years ago the restraints were still pernicious: family, church, community, school."

He was likely right on that point, Con knew. Though Nick's recollections of a century past were profound bullshit. Yet Con played along:

"Why didn't you ever write about Oak Park?"

Nick's jaw tightened. "I did not think a man should make money out of his father shooting himself nor out of his mother who drove him to it."

Con noted Nick's chest heaving and his eyes going glassy.

*

On Duval Street the perpetual party continued: nearly round-the-clock, three hundred sixty-five days a year except during hurricanes. Mondays pretty much the same as Saturdays: A band belting out blues in Sloppy Joe's. A nasally folk-singer at Jimmy Buffet's Margaritaville. Shops up and down the strip selling everything from alligator keychains to tee-shirts reading "Rehab's for quitters." Young men wearing fraternity tee-shirts staggered along the sidewalk eyeing women of all ages. A scrubbed young couple, honeymooners, perhaps, wearing matching polo shirts, stood hand-in-hand ogling dildos and leather harnesses in a shop window. Every day fresh replacements arrived by boat, bus, plane, and car, had their spree, then returned to their jobs, classrooms, husbands and wives.

The two men strolled over to Whitehead Street and down the block to the Green Parrot, where they got a couple gin-and-tonics. Nick stared off over the oval bar and through the open hurricane shutters to a two-story building across the street.

"Used to be a cathouse on that corner. Town was freer, cleaner, quieter. Makes me long for Idaho."

"I hear Hollywood's bought it up. You'd be elbow-to-asshole with human shields for grizzlies."

"The bastids. Shit, Conman, we're both getting our periods at the same time. Need to get off the rock for a while. I've got a proposition." Nick took a pull on his gin-and-tonic. "Nothing will change unless we do it ourselves. Like in the old days when you made your own rules and improvised everything—a good recipe for vivid living."

"What's your plan?"

Nick gazed off toward the southeast as if staring out to sea. "Got something waiting in Havana that could change everything, Conman." He took another drink. "Cuba," he said. "We'll take the Pilar to Cuba."

Chapter Seven

Con woke to another sunny day from fantastic dreams of the Cuban capital, wondering what the real Havana might hold for him. Maybe a story, a character, a setting, something that could grow into a novel. But he had no true idea, as Nick had been vague about the trip and his duties, saying only that he needed "help with a little cargo."

Con found himself out of coffee and so walked down the block to get an espresso. At the coffee shop the clerk's incompetence intrigued him. The guy moved as if in a trance and had to ask each customer twice for their order since halfway through fixing it he forgot what he was doing. Con had been observing a certain dissociation in many people he dealt with on the island, even sober ones. Virtually no one did what they promised, exhibiting super self-involvement and short attention-spans, as if all were on drugs. Often when Con spoke to them he sensed he was talking to himself, finding vacant eyes, non-responsive replies, and slack jaws. Or he got a lot of bullshit, people trying to sell him this or that, if only an excuse. He thought to ask Nick whether people had always behaved like that in

Key West, then caught himself.

After ten minutes he finally got his espresso and returned to his verandah to read Montaigne, far more accessible company than his contemporaries. "Que sais-je?"— What do I know?—the essayist asked, reminding Con to depend on his own judgment, to rely on himself.

Soon Johannsen telephoned asking whether he knew what day it was.

"Wednesday?"

"Factually correct but contextually non-responsive. First day of lobster season. Get your ass up here."

*

Con grabbed his lobster gear and bicycled up island on U.S 1, over Cow Key Channel, and on to Stock Island. He paralleled the chain-link out-of-bounds fence of Key West Country Club's fifth fairway and turned onto Key Haven, braking, after a half hour ride, by the concrete dock behind Johannsen's house. Con found him loading a cooler of beer and Cuban sandwiches onto Tailchaser, his twenty-four-foot powerboat. All of this—Johannsen's luxurious marital home, boat, and leisure—came from his ex-wife via a rancorous divorce. After the settlement, in a seeming gesture of spite, she donated millions to a political party he purportedly loathed. But Johannsen was in fact indifferent, comforted by the now peaceful sunset views from his second-storey deck overlooking the Gulf of Mexico and his affair with a Russian redhead, Nadya.

A twelve-knot southeasterly wind had stirred up the Atlantic, so they headed to the Gulf flats. The conditions on the island's leeside were fine, the shallow waters smooth and clear, the sun high and warming. On his GPS Johannsen punched in the location of a secret lobster hole where they had had success the previous season. They cruised through a winding channel toward Christmas Tree Island. But when they arrived at the spot, they found another boat already anchored there, dive flag flying. At two other spots he had recorded they found the same: Other divers had already beaten them to the lobsters.

As remedy, he sent Con over the side with his snorkel and a forty-foot line tied to the stern, to cruise the flats in hopes of finding the odd coral head or sponge forest where lobster lurked. Going over the side always thrilled Con, for he saw it as a potential leap down the food chain, recalling the Duck Key man who the previous week had lost his arm to a bull shark in the canal behind his house.

The water was warm, nearly ninety degrees Fahrenheit, and seemingly benign. Johannsen put the boat in gear, the line tightened, and off they went at three knots.

The flats were just that: a flat, sea-grass-and-sandy-bottomed shallows of vast proportions whose depth, depending on the tide and coordinates, ran from ankle-high on a blue heron to twenty feet. They cruised through six-to-ten-foot waters, a dream world of sea fans, sponges, gaudy tropical fish, grasses, and diffused glittering light. A silent world except for the rush of water in Con's ears and the sound of his own breathing, a largely pristine, natural wilderness, a calm and vivifying antidote to the concrete, noise, and angst of Key West.

Soon he glided over a large golden brain coral teeming with life, including a harmless six-foot nurse shark. Also yellowtail snapper, blue trigger fish, black-striped sergeant-majors, butterfly fish, and lobster, for he spied their antennae at the base of the coral. He dropped the line, called, and waved to Johannsen, who looked back, saw him waving, and brought the boat about, dropping anchor beside him. Johannsen tossed Con his lobster gear and followed him into the water.

They kicked down to the bottom to find a number of legal-looking bugs, as Conchs called them. The job now, while holding your breath and kicking to stay down, was to select a likely victim and, with the three-foot-long tickle-stick, prod him into the open, backing him toward the short-handled net in your other hand. Once you netted him you needed to grab the creature with the rubberized gloves (necessary to avoid ripping your hands on his spines), surface, and measure him to see if legal size. If so, you bagged him or tossed him in the boat. As Johannsen said, it wasn't picking apples but sport, for lobsters were fast, elusive swimmers who, unlike humans, didn't have to surface every minute to gulp air.

But this was a good hole, and after an hour of diving, wrestling lobsters, and swallowing water, each man had his limit of six legal crustaceans. They collapsed on Tailchaser's padded banquettes, lungs and legs aching. Johannsen pulled Heinekens and sandwiches from the cooler, and the two men lolled in the sun as they ate.

A hundred yards to the southwest lay a small, mangrove-covered key where snowy egrets perched, dotting the green island with white. The wind had eased. They sat on still, translucent, aquamarine waters, the hot sun at zenith.

Johannsen eyed the mangrove isle, studied the shining water, and drank from his beer bottle. "My parents' great ambition for me," he said, "was that I learn a trade—plumbing, perhaps—so I'd be my own boss and not have to work factory shifts like my father and grandfather. In other words, a life unclogging Milwaukee toilets."

"Lots of shit jobs out there. I had a Teamster card and hustled freight to get through grad school."

"Uplifting?"

"Prison sans sodomy." Con stared off at the horizon. "But we each build our own prison."

Beer in hand, Johannsen took a bite of his sandwich and studied Con. "You certainly can't be talking about yourself."

"I'm facing some issues, Jojo."

"Let's take stock: You're a healthy, forty-year-old male spending a Wednesday morning chasing lobster in the Gulf of Mexico and drinking beer. How can you endure such torture?"

"I was thinking of my writing. Maybe I've lost it."

"Relax. It'll surface again."

High in the southern sky Con saw vultures circling. "Wonder if it's related to the money problem."

"What money problem?"

"Pretty much tapped out and behind in the rent. But I've got something that could keep me going for a couple years. Though I'm reluctant to pull the trigger."

"What's the gig?"

"Eva offered me ten gees to marry her and play hubby. She cooks, cleans, pays half the rent, then walks away with her Green Card after two years."

Johannsen took another drink. "Let me get this straight: The hottest babe on the island, a twenty-eight-year old Czech pro, wants to keep you for two years no strings attached? Yes, I can see why you're agonizing."

Con fetched another beer from the cooler and pried off the cap. "And I've a second iron in the fire, five gees worth."

"For?"

"A trip to Cuba."

"To do what?"

"It's unclear."

"Someone trustworthy?"

"A guy who looks like Hemingway. He even talks like Hemingway."

"Through the hole blown in the top of his skull?"

"And get this: He also claims to be Hemingway reincarnate."

"Have you seen the whacko at Mallory Square who

says he's The Living Christ?"

"But this guy's believable: Looks, demeanor, intel-lect…"

Johannsen stared at him agape. "'This guy's believable.' That's rich, Con. You've been a year and already the sun and suds have steamed your brain. Or maybe Cat's bullet left you loony. Hemingway alive! Ha! Maybe you have lost it."

"Fuck you," Con countered. But he saw that this was what friends were for: ridicule and correction when you've headed off-course. But he really didn't know what course to take.

Chapter Eight

The new day came sunny and windless, though Con had been awake long before dawn thanks to a rooster that had perched in a sand tree outside his bedroom window and begun crowing at three a.m.

After breakfast he walked over to Nick's boat to check on plans for the Cuba trip. On the harbor boardwalk he saw a grimy man perhaps his own age draining off half-empty beer bottles leftover from the previous night. Con said a pagan prayer in passing, both for the bum and for himself. He was damn close to homelessness as well.

On the Pilar Nick was running new line on the outriggers. When Con asked about Havana, he said: "Bad weather."

Con looked around. The sky was clear, the water flat and blue. The Stars-and-Stripes aft hung limp. "Something brewing?"

Nick lifted his chin toward the Florida Straits. "Hurricane Francesca. Three days out. Could turn this way."

"Hell, that's my ex-wife's name. As a writer attuned to

ironic plot twists and cosmic justice, I see this as a terrific opportunity for a heavenly horselaugh at my expense."

Nick nodded. "Better keep an eye on her."

Con spied the copy of his novel sitting on the fantail. Nick followed his gaze there then refocused on the outrigger. "Read your book, Conman. You've got talent and sensitivity. And at times you're profound. You may even write a great novel someday. But that one ain't it."

Con glared at him. "The real Hemingway wrote some less-than-great books too."

"Name one."

"*Across the River and Into the Trees.* Self-absorbed and pretentious autobiography of his finger-fuck affair with that Croatian hustler."

Nick stared back, frozen.

Con went on: "And *The Old Man and the Sea* bored the hell out of me. I heard better fishing stories in the Ozarks. Not to mention the crude symbolism."

"There isn't any symbolism and all the talk about it is shit. The sea is the sea. The old man is an old man. The fish is a fish. The shark is like all sharks, no better and no worse."

"Then there was *For Whom the Bell Tolls*—emotionally flat and monotonous. Robert forever on the run with the taciturn wench, drinking bad wine and underestimating the Fascists. And the stilted English rendering of the Spanish made me laugh."

"Read it again."

"If thou suggests thus, I shall. That it will be a good read."

"Chinga tu madre."

"And *To Have and Have Not* was a hatchet job that Faulkner improved on with his screenplay."

"Faulkner! He wrote like an amnesiac, like he'd never read the book."

"He had to pull a narrative thread out of it somehow. Hemingway should have admitted it was a collection of short stories instead of trying to pass it off as a novel."

"The short story's art. But everyone wants a novel."

Con nodded thinking of his own best work, short stories published in obscure literary journals that virtually no one read, and what he had swallowed to get his novel published. But he pushed those darkening thoughts aside.

"If Hemingway had taken the time to write a real novel, layered, unified, and dovetailed in parallel stories, he'd have had something. But as it stands it's one of his lesser books. And his portrayal of the class struggle seems superficial."

Nick's eyes tightened. "I'd seen that life and death dance in Spain, Africa, even Paris. I myself fought through lean times."

"I don't know. Remember Hemingway was a rich doctor's son who never had to sell newspapers for his lunch money, never once had a real nine-to-five. Despite dubious claims about living off pigeons in Paris, he never had to worry about the small sums that beat you down."

Nick squinted at Con with fists clenched, as if itching to deck him. But after a moment he breathed out and seemed to soften. "All that's done. Dead and gone. All we can do now is see that you don't write any more shit. Sooner or later, Conman, you need to do something not clever and slick but real. To take a stand and live or die by it. I did not believe anyone could write any way except the very best he could write without destroying his talent."

Con felt perspiration beading on his neck as Nick's gaze penetrated him, as if he could see into his heart. Con knew his "success" had been tainted. He'd landed a hot agent—a former grad school colleague—who liked his facility with dialogue. She helped him recast his book, excising its complex "literary" elements, as she called them, and augmenting its tawdry ones, morphing it into a soulless page-turner. She then solicited insincere yet hyperbolic blurbs from bestselling authors in her stable and called in favors from New York critics. Soon everything fell into place. A page one rave in *The New York Times Sunday Book Review*. Other reviewers took their cue, marching lock-step in the parade of praise. *Sirens in the Street* flew up the bestseller list, Con migrating from obscure author of obscure short fiction to noted novelist in weeks, from pauper to spendthrift. So he knew he had gotten lucky, in a way. He knew, too, that he was a fraud. That his novel, as Nick pointed out, was not great literature but a gimmicky commercial endeavor. And that he had bitched himself by putting his name to second-rate stuff, by whoring.

However, he also believed he had better inside him, things he had not yet touched or lured out into his work. Con sensed that he just might be capable of creating something with true heart, a book with honesty and grace. But he didn't know how or where to begin. He had lost his compass and did not know what direction home.

Con spied a cooler near the helm and helped himself to a beer. He felt himself trembling with the acknowledged passion to write something fine—and the fear that he might not ever be able to pull it off. Sensing Nick's eyes still focused on him, he covered his emotional state with feigned bravado.

"Not ready to die. Let you know when."

Nick studied him. "You probably will live a long time thanks to your simpleminded optimism à la Candide. If sincere, an odd point of view for a writer."

"I know it's a flaw but I can't help it," Con said, lowering himself into the hammock strung under the bimini, swinging back and forth, back and forth. He knew that was bullshit. What optimism he'd had when young had been ground to self doubt over two decades. But he couldn't bring himself to admit it out loud. "I always cling to my mystic raft of redemption, believing in my ultimate vindication and well-being—though not holding high hopes for the rest of the benighted species."

Nick looked at him askance. "Wishing won't do it, Conman. Nor will hiding behind big words. Hard work needed. Follow my lead. Early on I started to break down my writing and get rid of all facility and try to make instead of describe. From then on writing was wonderful to do. But it was very difficult and took me all morning to write a paragraph. Couldn't see how I could ever write a novel. But that's the job, take it or leave it."

A gull standing on the dock squawked then flew when Con looked at it. "I'll write a great novel, Nick, soon as I fix myself," he said. "Nothing comes close to writing a book. It uses everything you got and stuff you didn't know you had."

"As near to heaven we get till we join the deads. I had to write to be happy whether I got paid for it or not. A hell of a disease to be born with. And I liked to do it, which was even worse. That made a disease into a vice. Then I wanted to do it better than anybody had ever done it, which made it into an obsession."

Nick's words hung in the air around Con as he swung, the earth seemingly swaying. Obsession: That described it. Con put a foot down on deck to arrest his movement and looked at Nick. "I have to do it, Nick."

"We'll set you back on track, Conman. I've got a plan."

*

Con spent the rest of the day at Fort Zach, lying under the pines reading, snorkeling out in warm, soup-like water that did not refresh, dozing on the beach. Near sunset he biked up to Bayview Park for tennis. But even with the sun down, the air hung hot and humid, and after two sets with Johannsen he was drenched and depleted. He went to the fountain on the side of the pro shop to refill his water bottle, and when he turned back to retreat to the courts, Cat stood before him.

He stopped and straightened, feeling his heart hitting heavy in his chest. She wore a light-gray business suit and high heels, and stepped toward him.

"I have something important to say."

The scent of her perfume—earthy and evocative of hot nights together—wafted to him, and he felt a ripple of desire cut across his solar plexus. But then, reminding himself of her ever-lurking and violent jealousy, he merely said, "Well?"

"First, I forgive you."

He took a step back. "You almost kill me and now you're the victim?"

"You cheated on me."

He held up his hand. "Did I ever ask what you did in Miami?"

She blanched and swallowed. "I was faithful to you."

"If you wanted that from me you should have negotiated it. You know the rules."

But he said it with little conviction, for he knew that women played for keeps, without rules, or at least with cryptic covenants that a guy had somehow to divine.

"I know I love you. That can't be negotiated. Don't you feel anything?"

"Lucky to be alive."

"That was an accident."

"No, a symptom. Not your first jealous rage."

She nodded and chewed her lip. "That's the second thing: I've changed. It won't happen again. Ever." The groan of an ambulance grew into a scream and Cat fell silent until it passed by behind her on U.S. 1. She folded her arms across her chest, as if to keep from embracing him. "We can have something beautiful together. Something special and enduring. It's what everyone wants."

"Not everyone. Some guys are gay and some are loners and some have a bit too much testosterone. I happen to fall in the third category, which is what attracted you in the first place."

She clenched her fists straight-armed at her sides as if wanting to pummel him. But then, as though with conscious effort, she relaxed. "We can work something out, Con. I know we can."

He'd thought he'd gotten over her—that's what he'd been telling himself. Logic told him to run but his heart told him otherwise, leaving him paralyzed.

But his dilemma was resolved by Johannsen appearing around the corner of the bleachers with his water bottle. Con introduced him to Cat, Jojo raising his eyebrows when he heard her name.

"Con told me about you."

"I can imagine."

"Here on vacation?"

"Down for the day on business." She looked to Con. "Stopped by on my way out to say hello."

He returned her gaze, still knotted up inside, still tongue-tied. "Hello then."

She nodded, turned, and retreated down the sidewalk, Con marking her retreat.

Chapter Nine

Pedaling home from the tennis courts that evening through the jasmine-scented night, Con felt cooled by the air pushing past him and contented by the quiet. Little traffic on Southard Street, stars overhead, queen palms and banyan trees standing guard along the way.

The scents of seasoned seafood and the ting of wine glasses touching came to him as he passed outdoor restaurants. The sound made him think of Cat and their beautiful moments together and wish that things had gone differently. Though he still felt that visceral thing for her, that mad wanting, he knew it was all wrong. Despite her claims he doubted very much that she would ever change, and would make his peaceful life hell on earth. That's what he was telling himself.

Back home, after locking his bike to the fence, he pushed through the front door and flipped the light switch for the stairs. But nothing happened. A blown bulb, he figured, and mounted the dark steps. At the top he sensed warm, still air and saw by the glow of streetlamps that the ceiling fans had stopped turning. He tried the lights in the kitchen without good result. Ditto in the bedroom. He went to the verandah, peered alongside the building to the downstairs windows, and saw light falling from them onto the short palms there. He marched downstairs with a flashlight and checked the circuit breakers outside. But he knew better. He was way behind on the rent, too.

Con retraced his steps upstairs, moved into the kitchen and pulled a beer from the dark but still cold refrigerator. He found a candle and matches and sat on a stool at the breakfast bar, sipping, staring at the flame, letting the situation sink in. His landlord and patron Berman wouldn't evict him but was too good a friend to stiff. So he had to do something—anything—to get some money.

From the fridge he took a piece of yellowtail snapper he'd planned to sauté for dinner, but the range was electric too. So he mixed up some wasabi and ate the fish raw, by candlelight. After a couple more beers he showered in the dark, dressed in cargoes, tank top, and flip-flops, and poured himself a dollop of rum in a plastic cup.

*

Downstairs to the sidewalk. He strolled aimlessly. Up Elizabeth Street to Solares Hill, down Angela Street toward the cemetery, mulling what to do next. A lightning flash in the distance illuminated a bank of clouds moving in from the east. He cut through the lane to Bill Butler Park, a small patch of unlit dirt umbrella-ed by banyans and coconut palms. A few raindrops began to fall through air smelling of ozone. More lightning sparked as he crossed the park. Then he sensed movement to his right. In the dark he perceived something slithering along the ground. He stepped back.

Close-set eyes stared at him from the blackness. Then with more lightning cracking close he spied a grit-and-tattoo-covered man. Barely distinguishable from the earth itself, he disappeared inside a cardboard refrigerator box lodged near a dumpster in the alley. Con stepped around the box, the eyes within it marking his movement. Con's heart pounded in dread, but not so much from the dark creature in the box but of a dark vision of his own future.

On Olivia Street the rain came harder. He turned right and moved back up Elizabeth toward home, his hand spidered over the plastic tumbler to prevent rain from diluting the rum. Ahead light shimmered on the wet walkway, and he saw that the doors of the Church of God of Prophecy once again stood open. As he neared, he heard the old women's voices rising in song—a hymn about the road to glory.

Glory. That was part of it at the beginning, he recalled. A necessary conceit, perhaps, that you were going to be the best damn writer of your generation—as Hemingway had vowed—that you'd leave your mark. But now all he wanted was to do the work, to recover the gift that he once felt surely had been granted him, to do true work that was his best.

He halted in the light of the church, a single-story, concrete-block structure. Con stood in the rain with his drink, mesmerized by the clear voices of the frail old women. The preacher sat at the piano pounding out chords. He spied Con in the doorway and, with a simple nod, beckoned him inside out of the rain. After a moment Con returned his nod, set his drink on the sidewalk under the eaves, and slid into the back pew.

Obscure images stirred his mind, thoughts of a dark, infertile future. Even direr feelings invaded his heart, fear of abandonment by the gods who once favored him.

The women sang another hymn, "Amazing Grace."

> Through many dangers, toils and snares,
> I have already come;
> 'Tis grace hath brought me safe thus far,
> And grace will lead me home.

Then the preacher rose and sent up a prayer, asking that God's grace guide and succor all those lost and suffering souls, and proffered a benediction.

The old black ladies filed past, opening umbrellas and bidding Con good evening. The preacher followed them to the door and stood beside Con, who looked up to study the old man. Thin and bald, with gray hair at the temples. A white shirt, thin gray tie, suspenders, gray slacks. His smooth skin, too, seemed almost gray. Con couldn't tell whether he was sixty-seven or ninety-seven.

"Thanks. You never know about lightning."

"You're always welcome here."

Con looked over his shoulder to see the rain still coming. "I'll wait a minute to see if it lets up. You ready to close?"

The man lowered himself in the pew across the aisle as if with effort, letting out a breath. "No hurry. Need to mop up." He squinted at Con. "Everything all right?"

"I'm okay." Lightning cracked nearby, causing Con once more to gaze behind him. He turned back and amended his response: "A little dispirited."

The preacher shook his head. "No spirit trouble is little."

"No, that's not it," he blurted and fell silent. He heard the rain drumming the roof.

Finally the old man said: "Want to talk about it?"

Con blew out a breath. "Not really. The usual stuff: finances, work, women."

"What kind of work?"

"I'm a writer. Or used to be." Con looked at the makeshift altar—a folding table covered with white brocade cloth—and the homemade wooden cross on the wall behind it. The preacher rested his hands in his lap, silent, waiting. Con shook his head. "For twenty years I put my heart and soul in it. Now it's gone."

"Is that important? Does that truly matter in your life?"

Con turned his head and stared at the preacher, thinking that was a damn good question, which made him think about what he really felt.

"It's all that matters. Without it, it's like a bad novel. No matter how fine the writing or how beautiful its moments, it never works if the core isn't solid, if it has no heart."

The man studied him. "I see."

"I don't care about the money. I'd do anything to survive if I could write something honest and solid." Con stared again at the wooden cross. "I don't want to waste my life."

"No life is wasted. We touch each other in many ways."

"That's not enough."

Con became aware that that was the sort of vain and sappy shit you'd never tell a friend. But he'd likely never see the old man again.

The preacher asked: "You have family?"

"Gone." Con shook his head. "So much goes into a person. Parents, teachers, friends do their bit. You strive to make yourself into the man you want to be. Everyone has high hopes for you, including yourself."

"And God."

Con grew conscious of the hollow sound of raindrops pooling on the sidewalk. "Then life happens. Bad choices and bad luck. A bad marriage and bad advice. Naiveté, stupidity, self-indulgence and self-pity. Lust, pride, envy, and other deadly sins. Before you know it you've betrayed yourself."

The old man stared at a hymnal on the pew beside him. "I wasted half my life. I see that now." He looked up to Con. "You still have time. Trust in God. Trust Him and be bold."

"How do you tell bold from foolhardy?"

"Follow your heart."

"Wish I had."

"Do you pray?"

Con shook his head.

"I'll pray for you. What's your name?"

The old man asked God's forgiveness for Constantine's transgressions and that he be filled with God, that he realize God and goodness resided within everyone. Con took it in, wondering why his gods had abandoned him. But then he caught himself and checked the self pity. He knew he had abandoned them.

Finally the old guy wrapped it up: "Bless him, Lord."

Outside it was still raining. Con grabbed his plastic cup from the sidewalk, drained off the rum, and made his way back to his darkened home.

Chapter Ten

The next evening as Con lounged on the verandah hammock reading a Hemingway biography, he heard the gate open and a knock on the downstairs door. When he descended and gazed through the screen he saw Nick in his beige fishing cap, puffing on his pipe.

"Fickle Francesca's turned south to embrace the Yucatán, Conman. Boosty's fixing things to shove off for Havana at dawn."

"Fits with my schedule."

They sat on the verandah sipping beer, the day cooling as the sun set. Con picked up his book. "Listen to this, Nick: Thurber claimed Hemingway's disintegration came from hiding the fact that he was 'gentle, understanding, sympathetic, compassionate.' And Gertrude Stein said: 'He had compensated for his incredibly acute shyness and sensitivity by adopting a shield of brutality. When this happened he lost touch with his true genius.'"

Nick took a pull on his beer. "Their words carry a warning for any writer, or anyone: To thine own self be true. And keep a steady course."

"Speaking of which, just the three of us going across?"

Nick shook his head. "You and me, Conman. Busta-mante's a good hand but I can't trust him in Havana. Last time, he disappeared for three days before I found him dead drunk in a cathouse. He thought he'd been gone a few hours."

"Time flies when you're having fun."

Nick reached over to retrieve Con's tennis racquet lean-ing beside the screen door and took a tentative backhand. "This isn't a pleasure trip, Conman. We'll be returning with some valuable cargo. But there's some risk."

Con leaned forward in his wicker armchair, literally on the edge of his seat. But then he again heard the gate open and Eva calling through the screen door. She came up the stairs, sauntered onto the verandah in her turquoise Capri pants, and presented Con a bottle of rum. After introduc-tions, she went off to the candlelit kitchen to fix mojitos, Nick watching as she exited.

"Over the years, Conman, I've learned how rare and wonderful is a truly beautiful tail: living sculpture that only the experienced cognoscente can appreciate, aware that not all art is in museums. Important not to wake up later and ask with a flash of rueful insight, 'Where are the great tails of yesteryear?' but to enjoy them now. Only the free man—perhaps poor in material things but rich in his ob-servations of nature—knows what I'm talking about. The world's asleep except for a few wandering spirits who are alert long before the cock crows."

Across the street in the library parking lot a rooster cried on cue.

Eva returned with drinks. Nick proposed a toast: "To the callipygous Eva."

Sensing that he'd paid her a compliment, she slid onto his lap. When he asked where she was from, she began a play-by-play of the Czechs' Velvet Revolution.

"We lose everything. But I come to Key Vest and find Cone."

"Lucky Cone."

Con nodded. Until recently, he'd always felt himself lucky, that beneficent gods were watching over him. He rapped with his knuckles thrice on the balustrade in hopes they were still near. Nick noted it and said:

"We'll need some good luck."

"With the weather?"

"Weather should be fine."

"With what then?"

Nick pursed his lips. Then he reached for his drink, drank it down and handed Eva the glass. "That was delicious, daughter. How about an encore?"

She bounced up and moved inside. Nick noted her departure and said:

"Writing and travel broaden your ass if not your mind and I like to write standing up."

"What were you saying about the trip?"

He turned back to Con. "This will be an adventure."

"What sort of adventure?"

"A voyage of faith, Conman. The less you know the better."

The library rooster again crowed, and Con looked down to it. Maybe it was time for him to wake up. To accede to a trip across with an eccentric and possibly insane salt claiming to be from the spirit world was bad enough. To do so without a clear explanation of their purpose and possible risks brought into doubt his own sanity.

"The whole thing's making me nervous, Nick."

Nick took his pipe from his shirt pocket, packed it down with his thumb, and lit it. At last he looked up through a mist of smoke. "Trust me. I'm here to help you."

Con nodded without conveying any agreement. "That's not enough."

Nick regarded Con thoughtfully. He looked left then right, leaned forward and whispered. "Atocha!"

*

Nick departed after another drink and Eva left at ten. But Con couldn't sleep. He worried over the creaky and temperamental Pilar and wondered about Nick's navigation skills—Con had thought Bustamante would be along. He also feared crossing ninety miles of open sea in the small boat, having heard stories of twenty-foot waves in the Gulf Stream and abandoned boats, as well as pirates. Further, Nick's vagueness about their mission—and his allusion to the sunken galleon Atocha—left Con with a troubling uncertainty. In sum, none of it was very reassuring, and he was having second thoughts about the whole expedition. But he knew he had to do something, anything, to get some money and get himself back to work, and maybe this was it, though he hadn't seen a dime of the promised five gees. Finally, after midnight, he slept, but his dreams were not good.

PART TWO: CUBA

Chapter Eleven

It was still dark as Con moved down the dock with his backpack toward the Pilar. The air hung humid and warm despite the long night. In a halo of electric light at the helm he saw Nick, pipe clenched in his teeth, studying a chart spread there, and the smells of gasoline and sweet tobacco came to him. When Nick heard Con's footfall on the boards, he looked up and squinted into the dark. Con moved into the circle of light and Nick said:

"You're early. Rooster give a wakeup call?"

"Pre-empted by the two-year-old bawling below." Con helped himself to coffee from Nick's thermos. "I feel for the guy. A bartender who doesn't get home till three then tends the kid all day while his wife's at work."

"There's a lesson for you."

"Truly. A daily reminder of how good I got it: peace, solitude and no supervision."

"Trying to talk yourself out of something?"

The coffee tasted good and strong, smelling of chocolate. "Eva has an offer on the table: ten large for two years of marriage and cohab to get her Green Card."

Nick looked up from the chart. "Remember, Conman: The writing and screwing and drinking all come from the same well. Make your choice."

"All three."

"If you're a writer you're in training. The big fight is now. To be champ you can't get lax in your regimen or stand flatfooted."

With that Nick turned back to the helm.

After a few coughing sputters the Pilar started, sending a mushroom of black smoke into the night sky. Con released the lines aft. They glided out into the harbor, moving past darkened vessels that dwarfed the Pilar, reminding him of how small they were, how big the sea.

*

Once outside the harbor they cruised past Mallory Square, the old submarine base, and Fort Zachary Taylor. Soon the lights of Key West were disappearing behind them as the sky lightened portside. Six miles out they got beyond the reef and the flat water morphed into three-foot swells. But the wind blew at a nice five knots and all was well. They fell quiet as the day brightened. The Gulf Stream rolled beneath them an unfathomable blue.

"Always amazed by the color," said Con. "Opaque and translucent at the same time."

"The Stream's a wonder," said Nick. "Greater than all the rivers in the world combined. And like all great forces ultimately unknowable."

Con studied a string of uninhabited mangrove-covered isles passing to starboard. Nick drank coffee. The Pilar purred. Con felt a warm breeze on his face and tasted salt-water spray on his lips. After a while he pulled from his backpack a Cuba guidebook from the library and cracked it open.

After a few minutes he looked up and said: "Guess how many sewage-treatment plants in Cuba."

"Zero."

"Good guess."

"The Commies can't put two dimes together since the Soviets tanked. Except for Fidel, who lives like a pasha. But whatever system you got ends up socialism for the rich and capitalism for the poor."

Con read on in the guidebook. "Lots of shipwrecks and pirates in the old days."

Nick gazed off toward the horizon. "Stacks of Spanish gold still out there. All you got to do is find it."

"And pirates?"

"In the Malacca Straits, not around here much. But you got to be ready."

"With cutlass and cannon?"

He looked at Con. "Come here, Conman."

Con followed him below. In the cabin Nick knelt in the bow and, beneath the bunk in the nose of the boat, removed a panel to reveal a compartment roomy enough for a substantial man. He reached in and withdrew a machine gun.

"Take her up for test firing."

Back on deck Nick stood feet spread in the stern and lifted the weapon. A sudden jerk of the gun and ear-splitting explosions. The weapon jumped in Nick's grasp, his shoulders shook, and Con saw a line of bullets breaking into the blue waves behind them.

Nick held the black gun out to him. "Try it. Just in case."

Con took it. "In case of what?"

"Blackbeard's ghost. Brace the stock here. There you go."

He fired off a few rounds that rattled his spine and left his ears ringing. But worse was the uncomfortable intuition that Nick was hiding a lot from him. Con handed back the weapon.

"What sort of cargo we hauling, Nick?"

Nick re-engaged the safety. "Better you don't know so it's my lookout and not yours. You're just a passenger. A writer doing research on a book set in Havana."

"You never know."

They putted along at ten knots. When the sun stood at zenith Con asked: "How much longer?"

"We're halfway. Slow going against the Gulf Stream. Faster coming back." He reached up and knocked on the wood panel encircling the dash.

Con surveyed the horizon, where the royal blue of the Gulf Stream met the pale blue sky. "Good to be away from landlubber concerns."

"Mulling the Czech's offer?"

"Yours was more compelling."

Nick unbuttoned the pocket of his khaki shirt and handed Con a short stack of folded hundred-dollar bills. "Here's a thousand on account. And on condition you won't get amnesia in a whorehouse like Boosty."

Con tucked the money into his jeans. "Not when they're giving it away in Key West."

"What you really need, Conman, is a rich woman. I had a few from St. Louie. Probably still some there."

"Francesca came from the same neighborhood as Hadley. Beautiful but high maintenance and no trust fund."

"A writer needs a woman with cash, not one who requires constant care and upkeep. An old-fashioned girl, possibly European."

"Any Old World Hemingways around? I was thinking of your German branch: a twenty-something Nietzschean with euros up the wazoo."

"Not interested in distant relatives or incestors. You know, the writing's best when you're in love. You write for two people: yourself, to try to make it absolutely perfect or at least wonderful, and for who you love, whether she can read or not and whether she's alive or dead."

Con nodded as an image of Cat floated across his consciousness. Nick went on:

"But marriage ain't always bliss, which undermines your work. Maybe your system's best, better even than the captain's paradise of a wife in every port: occasional companionship followed by pure solitude. I know that I always had to ease off the making love when writing hard as the two things are run by the same motor."

"Thank God for my turbocharger."

"Just remember that getting excessively passionate with a woman diminishes the passion for your work. Same goes for money or booze or whatever other passion. With me my work always came first. At least at the beginning. Some women understand that and are keepers. The others should be returned immediately to the stream."

Nick checked the compass and corrected course before continuing:

"It's a great mystery, Conman, why a woman will go to such lengths to find a man to suit her tastes—say, a man of high spirits, independence, and worldliness—work tirelessly to win his heart, and then, when she's done so, strive to strip him of his vitality and sovereignty, the exact things that attracted her in the first place."

"It is sport, like turkey hunting. They even wear camouflage and sound mating calls."

"Conversely, the solid, self-loving woman knows that the only way to keep her man and keep him whole is leave him be what he is. I know that my dramatic and thus addictive relations with certain women had a detrimental effect on me and my work, hamstringing me geographically and emotionally. Sadly, the great thing of value she possesses ultimately succumbs to oxidants or whatever, leaving a man with that same hollow feeling of loss and resignation he gets when a good set of tires finally wears out."

"Cynic."

"Since back when."

"I remember how you had Phillip ditch Dorothy in *The Fifth Column*. When she asks why he won't take her with him, he says, 'Because you're useless, really. You're uneducated, you're useless, you're a fool and you're lazy.'"

Nick gazed off as if going into the dream of the play. "She cries and alludes to her sexual talents, to which he replies, 'That's a commodity you shouldn't pay too high a price for.'"

He shook himself out of it. "Hell with it. 'But that was in another country; and besides, the wench is dead.'"

"Shakespeare, right?"

"Marlowe."

"You sure?"

"*The Jew of Malta*, act four."

Con caught himself. He sensed the wind in his face, the vibration and groan of the engine, and scents of sea and the moldy boat. Playing along with Nick and his Hemingway persona was one thing, but don't for an instant think he's anything other than some eccentric with Keys Disease. Yet playing make-believe was what writers did, right? If this man was an agent for good—and possibly of Con's deliverance—what difference did it make who he was? Con told himself: faith. A willful suspension of disbelief, required in every drama. Easy enough. That's what he had done with Cat (who was proving harder to ditch than Phillip's Dorothy). The signs of potentially violent jealousy were there right from the start…

*

He recalled the Friday morning a week after they met, when he got a phone call. On his caller I.D. he recognized the name of the Miami law firm from her business card: a group of downtown attorneys who kept Latin American crooks out of American jails.

"Constantine," she breathed. "I have to have you."

"Delighted. Who's calling?"

"I can drive down this afternoon, you bad boy."

"All yours, Cat. I just put three claw marks on my calendar."

Later, about six, he was on the verandah reading Chekhov—whose inconclusive short stories somehow gave Con hope for his own inconclusive life—when he heard the deep bass of a muffled motor idling below then ceasing. He rose from his hammock and peered over the rail. There she sat in a black Lexus with the top down, combing windblown blonde hair with her fingers. She looked up through dark sunglasses, a feline grin on her lips. On the seat beside her sat a bouquet of roses and a dark green bottle of Champagne.

He met her on the front porch and followed her up the stairs carrying the flowers and Champagne, a 2000 Lamiable Brut, which made him salivate. Halfway up, she stopped and lifted the back of her camel-colored skirt.

"These new stockings…," she said, pretending to adjust the left one and letting him glimpse her beige garter belt.

A couple hours later while she was showering he leafed through her unfinished manuscript, *Flesh and Blood*, which she had brought along. The writing wasn't bad, but he found a disturbing scene of bloody vengeance by a betrayed Mexicana who unmanned her unfaithful lover with a machete, a scene that should have warned any writer who understood the deep psychological wellsprings of literature. But it was just fiction, he told himself. Then she came from the bathroom in a short black skirt, pink tank-top that showed an inch of her bronzed stomach, diamond studs in her earlobes, and golden hair still somehow windblown, and he forgot all about it.

They walked around the corner and down the block

to the Marquesa, one of the island's pricier restaurants. But for Cat money seemed no object. With their grouper she ordered a hundred-dollar bottle of grand cru white Burgundy, a Batard-Montrachet, brought by a curvy young Czech. When she left, Cat said:

"She really looked you over."

"Who?"

"The sommelier or sommeliess. All the Eastern Block babes here look like models."

"Even my Ukrainian housemaid, like a model for a Russian tank."

They clinked glasses. "Tell me about your work, Con. What sort of students do you have?"

He sipped his wine sensing her apparent jealous streak and deciding how to prevaricate about all his female students.

"It's a mix. All sorts of subject matter and genres." Marta came first to mind. "One's a reporter working on a true crime tome about that gal they found in Sloppy Joe's dumpster last year."

"I recall."

"Then there's Sandra, an older lady, heiress and former consort of pop-stars and presidents, though nonpartisan. Now, years after kissing, she's telling."

"Dangerous dating a writer. I won't end up in your next book, will I?"

"Not unless you do something outrageous."

Cat smiled and stroked his thigh under the white tablecloth. "That's tempting."

"And I have a new student, a sexually voracious blonde who drives down from Miami bearing great wine and hot lingerie. She's the one who shows the most promise, both as a writer and a character. But I'll need to get to know her better, see how she lives."

Her eyes tightened. "This is how I prefer to live: sybaritically. That's all you need to know."

After the wine and a couple Hennessys, they both felt festive and so strolled down Southard Street toward the Green Parrot. When still half a block away they could hear a soul band playing, for the windowless bar always had its shutters open.

> Do you like good music?
> Yeah, yeah.
> Sweet soul music?
> Yeah, yeah.

The crowd had spilled out onto the street, patrons ringed the oval bar three deep, and the dance floor had expanded around adjacent pool tables. Con pushed through to the rail, ordered two rum punches, and felt eyes on him from across the bar. He looked up, and there stood Marta. When she saw she had his attention, she stuck out her tongue and licked lewdly. Con glanced over his shoulder to find Cat focused on the stage and the black soul singer there. He looked back to Marta shaking his head and wagging an admonishing finger. She winked and moved off.

Cat and Con pressed their plastic cups together and drank. As the song ended the crowd cheered and clapped. The band broke into a slow one:

> Can I change my mind?
> Can we start all over again?

Duh-dit-dee-dee, went a nice little guitar fill. A nice little sentiment as well, Con thought. How grand to be able to start over again—to correct errors, to mend regret, to take courage. To be able to edit one's life. Yeah, yeah.

Cat took his hand and led him onto the dance floor. Others' warm perspiring arms pressed against his. Her perfume mingled with aromas of beer, perspiration, citrus, and cigarette smoke. He felt the vibration of the bass move through him and with it, also vibrating, came a sensation of fundamental happiness, a solid glee at being alive, of having a woman in his arms, sweet music in his head, the sense of movement, the press of humanity, and the warm summer night all around him. And even if he couldn't start all over again, fuck it, he told himself. He'd take what he had had: a charmed life. So what if he was broke, blocked, and rudderless—that was all just abstract nonsense. Here and now, what he tasted and felt—not the past nor future nor any achievements great or otherwise—that's what mattered.

He turned with Cat in his arms and saw Marta in front of the bandstand, eyes closed, brown beer bottle clutched to her chest, swaying to the music. But then she opened her eyes, saw him staring, and came dancing toward him, sidling through the crush of flesh. He turned away. Soon he felt Marta behind him, rubbing up against him—surreptitiously, she believed. But then Cat's eyes widened. She released Con and stepped toward Marta.

"Hey, sister, back off!"

Marta started, looked to him, and spread her hands in a gesture of innocence. But the lawyer wasn't buying her plea. She got in Marta's face, noses almost touching.

"Don't give me that innocent shit. I saw what you were doing."

A tall, bearded, bearish man nearby moved to step between them.

"Easy, ladies. Let's just chill and enjoy the music."

Cat turned on him. "None of your fucking business, buddy, so butt out."

He looked to Con, shaking his head. "She's all yours."

Marta meanwhile had retreated, melting into the crowd. At the bar Con knocked back his rum punch and got another. Cat stood rigid beside him playing twenty questions:

"Who's that woman?...Where do you know her from?... Why'd you let her do that?...You liked it, didn't you?"

But he knew instinctively that no words could soothe

her. So he leaned across and sunk his teeth into the back of her neck, as a wildcat did when doing its mate. Her shoulders sagged, her eyes closed. She leaned into him and breathed: "You make me crazy."

"Apparently."

But Con saw he had been just as crazy. At that point any rational animal would turn tail. But it was all so good— the aesthetics were just right and fate seemed to be lending a hand. He was falling for her.

Chapter Twelve

Their first sign of Cuban sovereignty came via one of Fidel's gunboats in menacing gray that approached to take a look at them. It cruised past fifty yards distant, cutting a thick V in the blue water, making Con feel vulnerable and even more at sea than he already did. Then on the horizon ahead he spied a growing nondescript shape. It morphed into beige buildings: Havana.

At the Marina Hemingway a uniformed customs officer tossed Con a line on the portside. He secured the Pilar as Nick killed the engine. Another officer in pressed white uniform shirt and dark trousers came from the concrete-block customs shed with a clipboard. Nick bid them both, "Buenas tardes," and invited them aboard. Their Cuban dialect, Con noted, was nothing like the Spanish he had learned in Mexico, but he'd already been acquainted with it in Key West.

In the cabin Nick mixed a shaker of daiquiris, poured out four glasses, and invited the officer with clipboard to sit on the bunk above the machine gun. He introduced himself as Nick Adams—the name of Hemingway's early autobiographical protagonist—and added, "This is the famous American writer Constantine Martens."

"¿De veras?" asked Javier, the man with clipboard, as if he'd actually heard of Con.

"Here is his most famous work."

Nick took his copy of *Sirens in the Streets* from his bookshelf and handed it to Javier, who leafed through it and passed it to his partner, Rafael. Rafael studied Con's photo on the dust jacket, held it up to compare it to his mug, and nodded.

Nick asked: "¿Puede usted leer inglés, Rafael?"

"No, lo siento. My wife is the English student. I am better with Russian."

"Take it with you," said Nick, pouring more liquor into Rafael's glass. "A gift for your wife."

"It is your personal copy."

"Por favor," Con interjected, sensing his cue to join in the massaging of the Cubans. "As a token of the ongoing amistad between our peoples."

"True, the people of Cuba and the United States of America will always be friends. I will borrow the book for her to read and return it when you leave."

"While we are at the marina," Nick said, "you are both invited to come aboard at anytime and relax with a cocktail. Mi barca es tu barca."

Javier and Rafael laughed.

After two daiquiris apiece they conducted a cursory inspection of the boat, pocketed Con's and Nick's customs declarations, stamped their passports, and directed them to a slip in the vast marina.

Con wondered about Nick's passport and what it might tell him. Then he caught himself. This was a voyage of faith. And no matter what it might have said, it would have proved nothing.

*

The sun had set by the time they tied up and connected the utilities. Both felt famished but too tired to head into Havana proper for dinner. However, they spied a returning Cuban fishing boat whose crew was happy to trade a wahoo for a couple American boating magazines.

While Nick and Con were grilling the fish aft, Javier showed up, calling to them from the dark. They shared their fish and beer with him, sitting on canvas deckchairs talking fishing, weather—another tropical depression was forming off Africa—and politics. The last rather obliquely, for Javier never referred to Castro by name, instead stroking an imaginary beard to indicate *El Líder*.

Javier himself was clean-shaven, forty-five, with dark, intelligent eyes behind steel-rimmed glasses. Con thought he looked like an assistant professor. After they had polished off a dozen beers and Nick headed below for a bottle of rum, Javier turned to Con and asked:

"¿Es difícil, no?"

"Is what difficult?"

"To write a book that people will read."

"Muy difícil."

"Yo entiendo, for I am working on a book."

Nick came up the gangway to catch that last bit and gave Con a meaningful look.

"Tell us about it, Javier."

"Es un cuento de amor…," a love story set in the late 1980's, he explained, about a Cubana who falls in love with a visiting East German political-science professor. They marry and settle in East Berlin, where she is content with her role as hausfrau and mother of their infant daughter. But when the Wall comes down her husband is seduced by capitalistic decadence, becoming grasping and superficial as well as a minor celebrity, commenting on politics for West German TV. Ultimately she leaves her husband and returns to Cuba with their daughter to raise her at the bosom of the Ongoing Revolution, thus saving her from corruption.

"Una buena idea," Con said. "When will you finish?"

"With a job and family it is difficult to find the time to write."

"Why not ask El Líder for a sabbatical?"

Javier suppressed a smile. He went on to ask Con technical questions about structure, character, and dialogue. Con answered them at length as Nick looked on silently, puffing on his pipe and pouring them more rum when they needed it. Con even threw in a quote from *Death in the Afternoon*, about a writer omitting things he knew: "'The dignity of movement of an iceberg is due to only one ninth of it being above water.'"

Nick gazed off the starboard side toward the night sea, eyes seemingly unfocused, and Con wondered if he was listening. Even after they finished the bottle and Javier bid them, "Buenas noches," Nick seemed distracted. Finally, as they sat studying the dark, star-littered sky, he spoke:

"To produce a work of art, Conman, you need to be an artist. To write something worthwhile, you need to live as a writer. Which means you should treat your life as if it's a novel you're writing. Unexpected characters and unforeseen events will show up and change your master plan, so it's up to you to adjust for the right emphasis. And your protagonist, whom you should know very well, won't always perform as expected, will indeed waver. But you must keep him in character and on the right track.

"Along the way, like Odysseus, you will intersect with certain attractive forces who believe the present is important and permanent. Remind yourself that it's your story not theirs and you have other objectives. The key is to keep the story moving forward and to be good to your hero."

Nick took a draw on his pipe. "Everything you produce, fact or fiction, won't necessarily be remembered or even noted. Only style and personal truth matter, and then only while you last."

With that he got up and went below, leaving Con alone with the night.

A strip of moonlight lay on the black, undulating water like an inviting yet treacherous road to heaven. To live one's life as a work of art. Nick was right, Con knew. A life thus with structure, drama, revelation, climax, denouement, and meaning. With integrity and submission to the requirements of the form. With balance, subtlety, pointed dialogue, irony, and some unexpected plot twists. And just maybe a happy ending, if you wanted to go Hollywood with it. But most important, an Odyssean hero who after years of wandering and struggling against monsters and sirens finds his way home and conquers his enemies, vanquishing all false suitors. Yes, that's the way to live it, Con saw, like he was the hero of his own life.

Chapter Thirteen

Con woke from a miraculous dream. In it an image came to him, vague, watery, then clearer, as though rising from the depths of the Gulf Stream: a mermaid with flowing black hair, beseeching smile, and Gulf Stream-blue eyes. He reached out to pull her on board, grasped her hand in his, and realized he was naked. She beckoned him into the water. "Venga," she said. "Ven acá."

Nick had hot coffee awaiting him in a thermos on the fantail but was nowhere to be found. An hour later an old Plymouth taxi with enormous tail fins, a remnant of the 'fifties, came smoking down the sunlit pier and halted beside the Pilar. Nick emerged from the back seat followed by a Cuban boy of perhaps twelve. Nick laid a hand on the boy's shoulder.

"Cuida la barca con tu vida, Marcos...Guard the boat with your life. Let no one pass. If anyone tries, show them this: a letter from Cuban customs officials saying the boat is under quarantine. Si hay problema, run to the customs office and get Señor Javier. ¿Entiendes?"

The boy nodded and stood before the boat like a sentry.

"You may sit on the boat, Marcos, in the shade."

The boy studied the Pilar then gazed across the harbor toward the customs shed. There a gray Navy gunboat sat moored, its uniformed officers milling about on the pier. "One is not able. One ought not go on the boats of foreigners."

Nick fetched Marcos a deckchair, sandwich, water bottle, and black umbrella. To Con he said: "Empty your backpack and bring it along."

*

Con slipped into the backseat of the taxi beside Nick. Soon they were motoring down a broad, tree-lined avenue of stately old homes, now fallen into disrepair and cut up into apartments. Laundry hung off balconies and children squatted in dusty yards.

Further on they came to well-kept properties: The Swiss Embassy slid past, then the Italian. As the cabbie raced through an intersection, a black man stepped from the curb into their path. The cabbie swerved the old Plymouth and laid on the horn. Once safely past, he looked to his passengers in the rearview mirror and reached up to touch his forearm with his other hand, as if to indicate the pedestrian's color.

Con said to Nick: "I see why the Revolution's Ongoing."

At Nick's instruction the driver dropped them on the Malecón. They strolled along the seawall and saw men fishing as Key West Cubans did, with spools of line and no rod, slinging the bait out from shore. They turned up the Avenida Italia to head toward the *centro*. Missing paving stones pocked the streets and sidewalks. The facades of once elegant buildings literally crumbled. A musty smell permeated the city's still air, as if an emblem of its decay.

"No mistaking Havana for Barcelona," Con said, "or any other city not under bombardment. If this is the center of the capital, I wonder what the hinterlands look like."

Nick nodded. "As the Old Chief once said, 'Long time ago good, now heap shit.'"

Everywhere lines of people waited for buses. Traffic was sparse. A young woman in jeans and white tee-shirt approached Con, rubbing her breasts. "One dollar," she said in accented English. "One dollar."

Others accosted them as they strolled, offering cigars, lodging, home-cooked meals, or sex, or asking for a hand-out.

"I thought that in the Workers' Paradise the people would be, well, working."

"The Triumph of the Revolution," said Nick, "is that instead of whoring the girls out to Americans they whore them out to Canucks and Krauts."

He led Con up the hill and through a grimy park to a corner tavern, El Castillo de Fames. At the bar sat two men with cameras chatting in Italian and sipping beer. Nick and Con ordered the same. When the bartender returned with two bottles of Cristal, Nick said to him: "Soy un amigo buscando a Ricardo Avila."

"¿Avila? No lo conozco."

"Sí, yo entiendo. But I would like to buy him a drink in the name of international brotherhood."

"The name means nothing to me."

Nick soon drained off his beer and slid the bartender a sawbuck.

"Tell him Nick Adams will return this evening."

*

Con followed Nick into Habana Vieja, the old town. There they walked narrow cobbled streets, buildings cheek-to-jowl along either side. As they passed a department store, Con looked inside to find a few bolts of checked cloth, the odd kitchen implement, empty shelves. On the street an intelligent-looking, fiftyish man in threadbare suit handed Nick a card. "If the señores need a place to stay, I have a furnished room at a good price."

A teenage mulata in a red lycra unitard flashed her eyes from a doorway as they passed and bid Con, "Hola, guapo."

"Why do they come onto me," he asked Nick, "and not you?"

"It's the blond hair and mustache, Conman. They think you're a Swede here for a Cuban experience."

Con turned back to wave goodbye as they walked on. "For the likes of her a trip from Stockholm might be worth it."

"You never know about Latin girls. American women the best lays."

"Can't argue there," he said, thinking of Cat, "but the least tractable."

"Your sample's bad. You attract man-eaters. Take a shot at one of these Cuban gals—a civilian not a hooker. Pass her a live grenade and see how she handles it. Good research for your next novel. Consider it all as research. That way you keep your distance and it stays malleable so you can use it like clay and make with it what you want."

Nick spread his hands and gestured if to indicate his total environs. "Look at this dramatic material: The failed revolution. The embargo. The fear and stupidity of the gringo government. The corruption and viciousness of the Castro regime. The banks and families who lost out fifty years ago still trying to fuck Fidel. El Líder putting professors in prison and driving others to flee in bathtubs. The ones who stay behind pimping out their kids for euros. It's a chickenshit deal all around that makes you want to resign your commission in the human race. But the world's always been a fucked up place."

"Great title for a world history: 'A Fucked-Up Place.' Reveals why I have such trouble fitting in."

"At least you're keeping your own vision."

"That's all a guy's got."

"I'll drink to that," Nick said, leading him into a small, dark tavern.

*

A chicken sandwich and three beers later they emerged into the hot late-afternoon.

"Time to kill," said Nick. "Shall we visit Granma?"

"Sure, if she runs a cathouse."

Nick guided him back up the hill to a small green park and the Museo de la Revolucíon. There preserved behind glass sat the motor yacht Granma, an icon of the National War of Liberation. In 1956 Fidel and a few fellow exiles bought it from an American in Mexico and sailed it across the Gulf. They landed on Cuban soil December 2 and headed for the hills of Sierra Maestra. Two years later Cuba would be theirs.

The museum also held tanks and prop planes from the war as well as pliers, can-openers, and other household items that Batista's men had purportedly used on the genitals of state enemies. Con stood studying the implements, feeling lightheaded. "Remember asking if I can keep my mouth shut?"

"Name, rank, and serial number, Conman, even if they clamp your cojones."

"This shit's making me queasy, Nick. I need a drink."

*

They moved on to a bar that boasted a framed photo of Fidel and an older Hemingway shaking hands. Hanging on the wall next to it a poster announced the annual Ernest Hemingway International Game Fishing Tournament.

"Just missed the tourney."

Nick looked askance at the poster and shook his head.

"Can't blame them. Desperate for dollars. A poor and hungry people. And fearful." Nick made the sign of the beard. "Bastard expropriated the Finca along with my library."

The bartender came with their mojitos, bowed, and moved away.

"Is that what we're here for, Nick, to liberate Cubans?"

Nick took a sip and licked his lips. "Just one. But in turn he could free us both."

However, that cryptic phrase was all Nick had to say on the topic, and he soon engaged the bartender in talk about Cuban ballplayers.

When the sun set they headed up the sidewalk in the direction of the Castillo de Fames. The unlit streets of Havana seemed so surreal to Con, what with the crumbling buildings and the blank-faced people idling about. A man approached out of the dark selling pesos. Con waved him away.

"I prefer Key West, Nick: decadence over decay. Though I feel a certain kinship with Fidel: He can't pay his electric bill either."

Nick just nodded, his mind elsewhere.

Lightning cracked overhead followed by a sudden warm rain as they reached the tavern door. They ordered two beers as the bar began filling with streetwalkers and pimps dodging the downpour.

A young man smelling of perspiration took the barstool next to Con, introduced himself as Alberto, and asked if he'd like a *jintera*, lifting his chin toward a trio of mini-skirted teenagers racing through the door giggling and shaking rainwater from their black, curling hair. Model thin, the youngest looked twelve or thirteen, the other two perhaps sixteen.

"No, gracias," Con told him. "I am a priest."

The man laughed and asked where he was from. When Con told him Key West, the pimp nodded and gazed out the window to the dark street in the direction of the Florida Straits. "Ay, Cayo Hueso. I have rich cousins there. There everyone is rich."

Nick talked up two older whores, maybe twenty-five each, as Alberto went on: "I labor all day in a factory, work the streets at night, and still must live with my mother. I can't even afford a beer."

Con signaled the bartender, who brought Alberto a Cristal, and the two men knocked bottles together. "To the Ongoing Revolution," said Con, and Alberto smiled ruefully.

He borrowed pen and paper from Con. "Here are my cousins in Key West and my address in Habana. Tell them they can visit anytime."

Alberto rambled on, talking about how he wanted to study medicine but had no connections to get him out of the factory. And how, if he could get to America, he would become a doctor and help poor people everywhere. Then Con saw his eyes fix on the door and tighten. He followed Alberto's gaze to a lean, square-shouldered Cuban in a dark raincoat paused in the doorway, seemingly staring at them. The man moved toward Con but then stopped and laid a hand on Nick's shoulder. Nick turned.

"Ricardo!"

The two men shook hands. Nick introduced Con and bought another round. Then the three of them took their beers to a table in the corner as the bartender turned up the volume on a radio playing tango music.

"¿Cómo fue tu viaje, Nicholas?"

"The trip across went fine, Ricardo. The Pilar's a steady boat," Nick said, knocking thrice on the wooden tabletop. "You have everything?"

"Todo. I am ready."

"All is well with the cargo?"

"When I got the message that you were here I returned

for the charts."

Con looked at Nick, but he did not return his gaze.

"Where are they?"

"En la casa de mi hermana." He looked at his dive watch. "She finishes work at ten. We can get them then."

Chapter Fourteen

When the rain stopped they walked back down the hill into Old Havana, the damp-smelling streets dark and quiet, the only light coming from open doorways and windows where an occasional electric fan turned. The fragrances of frying garlic and jasmine came on a sudden breeze from the sea. Distant thunder made Ricardo look up at the black sky.

"Rainy season. Showers are normal. But I am worried about a storm off Jamaica. But it should not strike until late tomorrow."

"We'll beat it out."

At the bottom of the hill light fell onto the cobbled street from an old building where recorded music wafted out an open door and windows. Ricardo led them through the doorway to the right of which, inlaid in the stucco, a plaque read "Casa de Tango."

An older woman in black silk dress, high heels, and costume jewelry showed them to a rustic table in a crowded cabaret. After they ordered more beer from her, Ricardo turned to Con. "How do you pass your time in the United States?"

"I write novels and help other writers."

"One must always give back."

"Y tú, Ricardo, what do you do?"

Ricardo flicked his eyes at Nick.

"Está bien," Nick said. "We're all comrades here."

Ricardo turned back to Con. "I am an officer in the Cuban Navy."

"On a big ship?"

"No. Special forces, like your Navy Seals."

"You sound dangerous."

"I could be if we had enemies other than ourselves. For now, the Navy employs me as a salvage diver."

Three gray-haired men mounted a low stage where rested an upright bass, accordion, and guitar. The recorded music died, lights dimmed, and a single spotlight focused Con's attention on the combo. At once they began playing a slow, rhythmic song. Soon the woman in the black dress stepped to the stage and began to sing, projecting a clear voice throughout the room without aid of a microphone. After a few seconds couples rose from their tables and gathered on the small dance floor before the bandstand. They moved to the music with sensual dignity, elegant and erect. An Argentine invention, the tango, Con knew. A way to dance out your eroticism and sadness, which fit Cuba. His beer tasted bittersweet and he felt like he had time-traveled to a purer place.

The song ended, the dancers applauded. After another song and more applause the old woman stepped forward bowing. She introduced the musicians and thanked the National Council for Culture for its support of traditional music and the Casa de Tango.

"Permit me to introduce the petite cantante with the big voice, Aurora Avila."

Ricardo leaned toward Con as they clapped. "My sister."

Sweeping from the dark wings of the cabaret in flowered skirt and black strapless top came a slender woman with curling black hair and flaring nostrils. She looked like a dark goddess, fluid and formidable. She bowed to acknowledge the applause and turned to the accordion player, who counted aloud, "Uno, dos, tres," and the combo broke into a lilting Latin song. When she turned back and Con gazed upon her face fully for the first time, he started and felt his pulse quicken. For it was the woman from his dream, seemingly, the dark mermaid with Gulf Stream-blue eyes.

He sat hypnotized. Aurora: goddess of the dawn. Her voice came confident, strong, and penetrating. He felt it infecting and warming him like a fever, and told himself that he was a fool, that after all the beautiful women he'd known, here he was reacting like a schoolboy. But he couldn't help it. He felt as if he'd been stung. Worse, it wasn't honest lust but something weird and buzzy, as if he'd always carried an image of her inside him.

Others began again to dance. The previous singer came to their table and Nick rose to escort her onto the dance floor. But Con couldn't take his eyes from Aurora, who sang of great passion, lost love, and loneliness. She moved near their table to touch Ricardo's shoulder as she sang, and her scent, jasmine and musk, came to Con. On her pulsing throat he saw a necklace of cowrie shells. He watched as she moved away and sensed Ricardo's eyes on him.

She sang three songs during which Con spoke not a word. Then she bowed and came to sit.

"Cantas más melodioso que los pájaros," he said without calculation—you sing more sweetly than the birds.

"Gracias. But it is such old-fashioned music. Do you really like it?"

"En serio. Qué bella."

Ricardo introduced first Con then Nick. When she

heard the latter's name, Con saw her tense.

Nick ordered beer all around. "This is the way Habana used to be: Clubs everywhere where you could hear good music and dance."

Aurora turned to him. "Ricardo has told me of you, Señor Adams. I know why you have returned."

Her brother reached across to lay a hand on hers. "No te preocupes, Aurora. It will be well."

"Claro. I know this is right." She returned her gaze to Nick. "But Ricardo is the only family I have."

What with the surreality of Havana, being stung by Aurora, and sensing that Nick had been far less than forth-coming, Con felt at sea. He figured it showed, for Nick looked at him and said in English: "I'll tell you everything, Conman, soon. I ain't taking you where you don't want to go."

*

The four of them finished their beers and walked down the middle of the dark street, the other two men ahead, Con and Aurora following side-by-side. No cars passed. The night air lay warm and quiet around them.

"I have heard that Key West is beautiful."

"Sí, in places. But noisier and more dangerous than Havana."

"Here we have safe streets. There is that."

At a dark corner Aurora led them through the doors of a decrepit hotel. Over the dim doorway embossed on the crumbling Italianate façade Con could read "Palacio Vien-na." Inside, a lone bulb hanging by its cord lit an unswept lobby where an ornate brass elevator cage, once no doubt an elegant conveyance, sat disused, the metal now pitted and covered with dust. They followed Aurora up a bare wooden staircase, paint long ago worn away, banister gone.

They ascended as if climbing circles of Hell. Water dripped from a broken skylight in the center of the building. In the hallways women sat and smoked disconsolately; men played cards, eyeing the foreigners with suspicion. Above, a child twirled about a wooden column where the banister had rotted or been looted, unconcerned with the possibility of dropping three floors to her death. Smells of garlic and dust rose to Con's nostrils. All was gray except for the brightly colored cotton dresses and unitards of the smoking women.

On the third floor another group of shirtless men played cards at a low table. One sat up straight on his over-turned plastic bucket when he saw them. He yelled at Aurora:

"¡Sácate! It is against regulations to carry yumas to your home. You will pay."

Con looked to Nick. "'Yumas'?"

"Foreigners. The guy's likely the local Party snitch."

The other card players joined in the admonition. Con heard "pepes," Cuban for "johns." Aurora ignored their taunts and kept climbing but Ricardo stopped to cast them a hard look and they quieted.

Nick leaned toward Con. "Orwell would love this."

On the fourth floor Aurora stopped before a door secured by two padlocks. Soon she stepped through it and flipped on a light. A solitary room with cooking ring, kitchen table, and single bed. The artwork on the peeling walls consisted of pictures cut from magazines—the Alps, Paris, Madrid. Aurora turned to him.

"I have tried to grow plants but there is no sun."

She offered them tea. While the water heated on the burner, Con overheard Ricardo question Aurora about her visit that day to the clinic. She nodded and laid a hand on his. "My health is good."

Ricardo went to the narrow bed, bent and pulled from beneath it a black plastic sack. From it he withdrew long rolls of yellowed paper, which he spread on the table, using books as paperweights. The men bent over the top one, which, Con saw, was a nautical chart.

"Aquí, por ejemplo," Ricardo said, pointing, "is a wreck we worked for two months, finding a number of Spanish coins before being ordered to another site. But the manifest indicates gold bars. They are still there."

Con looked to Nick, who squinted at the chart. Now at last it was making sense. The human cargo they were to liberate came with charts that could lead to another Atocha. Treasure. Exactly what he needed.

When the tea was ready Ricardo pushed the charts aside. He and Nick sat on the only two chairs, whispering. Con sat beside Aurora on the bed as she gazed at the rolled charts on the table.

"You are close to your brother?"

"When our mother died he took care of me, ever since I was eight."

"Y tu padre. ¿Dónde está?"

"Ricardo's father died in prison. My father returned to Moscow. I did not know him."

Con sipped his tea and studied her, feeling stirred by her nearness. She asked: "Do you know Cuba?"

"This is my first trip."

"Havana is not Cuba. To know my country you must see the countryside."

"I wish I had more time to do so."

"You will return. When you do I will show it to you."

Nick called, "Conman, bring me your backpack." Con retrieved it from the floor beside him. Nick and Ricardo folded the charts flat and placed them inside.

They thanked Aurora for the tea, and Ricardo grabbed his raincoat. Con shook hands with Aurora, who stood on tiptoe to plant a kiss on either cheek, her scent again cutting through him.

"Buena suerte," she whispered. "Vaya con dios."

They found a taxi on the Malecón and dropped Ricardo a few blocks from his barracks. "Pues, hasta mañana," Nick said. "As planned."

*

Back at the Marina Hemingway Marcos lay curled on the dock before the Pilar's gangway. Nick shook him, paid him, and sent him home in the cab. Once on board, Nick stowed the charts beneath the bunk below and on deck poured them each a shot of rum while Con opened two beers.

"You got the drift, Conman?"

"We're taking him and the charts with us."

"Should be easy." Nick lowered himself into a deck-chair. "Tomorrow after dark we check through customs to head back. Tell them we're having engine trouble and may stop to make repairs offshore if it acts up. Half mile out we throttle down at the channel marker that Ricardo has swum to. We pull him aboard—your job—while I watch for Commies and keep the Pilar purring. You stow him below with the charts. Once outside the twelve-mile limit we're home free."

Con moved his jaw laterally, taking it all in, feeling his blood run cold despite the rum and warm evening. He nodded. "And if we get caught?"

"Cubans would confiscate the Pilar and arrest me for smuggling."

"Not to mention stealing government property."

"But you get off the hook: Claim ignorance and I back you."

"If they swallow it. Otherwise I land in the bote with you."

"I can use you, Conman. But if you say 'No,' I won't hold it against you. I wasn't square upfront."

Con paced the deck, eyes moving side to side. "Fucking A. Let's see: five gees for five years in Cuban prison.

You think I was that desperate?"

Nick looked at him. He opened his mouth to speak then checked himself. Finally he said: "You can find someone at the marina to run you back. Lots of American and Canuck boats off for the Keys every day."

"Let me sleep on it while you count doubloons in your dreams."

"Some treasure in it for you as well, Conman. But whatever you decide, I pay you the other four gees tomorrow." Nick drank down the rum and chased it with beer. "Yet more to it than money. Particularly for Ricardo."

"I'm listening."

"Neck's in a noose. Tried to blow the whistle on politicos skimming treasure. But apparently The Beard's helping himself as well. Nothing Ricardo can do. No free press, nothing. He'll end up in prison if he stays."

"So it's a charity gig?"

Nick's eyes shone in the cockpit light as he poured himself another rum. "No, Conman. I'm doing it for me and you. Trust me."

"The Key West mantra, commonly translated as 'bend over.' What's the Cuban phrase for that so I'll know it when I get to prison?"

"Overdramatic, Conman. All will go well."

"Yeah: 'Trust me.'"

"One more thing."

"Can't wait to hear."

"We're running against American law too. But my lookout not yours. Even if we dodge the Cubans I could lose the boat on the other end if caught and pay a stiff fine. But I got it fixed."

"Do tell."

"U.S. Customs uses the honor system. Easy to slip in, drop cargo, then call Immigration. Ricardo lies low for a few days with Boosty then surrenders to the nearest cop, saying his boat sunk offshore, and asks for asylum."

"Jesus."

"Do pray, Conman. Órale."

A warm, airless night, too hot to sleep below. Con pulled the mattress from the cabin bunk and placed it on deck portside, opposite Nick's hammock.

He figured to lie awake half the night thinking on what to do. But after a long day of drinking, he was asleep within minutes, dreaming of tropical storms, confused waters, and the woman with the Gulf Stream-blue eyes.

Chapter Fifteen

Con woke to a cool, dim morning. A band of yellow-gray clouds had moved in overnight and a stiff breeze whistled along the Pilar's canvas bimini. He spied white-caps on the gray water outside the marina. The air smelled different, musty, as if blowing easterly from the capital. Nick had gone. Con made coffee on the electric range in the galley and sat on deck sipping and reading Dos Passos's *Manhattan Transfer* from Nick's library.

It reminded him that the lasting American writers from Hemingway's generation were worldly sorts—journalists, soldiers, doctors, travelers—out among the people, taking risks, earning their stripes, finding their material. Well, here was his chance, he thought. A minor skirmish in the lingering Cold War. For a seeming good cause and a good friend—Nick had certainly been that to him. He balked at the thought of stiffing him and appearing chickenshit in Nick's eyes. Never underestimate the male fear of appearing chickenshit, he told himself. You could bet Nick was counting on it.

But from what he knew of Cuban prisons, he was right to feel scared. And he knew he shouldn't worry about stiffing Nick, who had manipulated him into a situation he never would have gotten into otherwise. Contemplating risking his freedom for five gees showed Con how desperate he'd become. Though maybe there was more: maybe some real treasure—of whatever sort—if he hung in… Thus went his inner dialog much of the morning.

At noon a Fiat taxi stopped beside the Pilar. Nick pried himself from the back seat and, from the trunk, unloaded food, ice, and beer for the trip back. After they stowed it away Nick said: "I'll stay with the boat if you've got somewhere to go."

But he didn't. He was too focused on his dilemma to think about sightseeing. Con strolled around the marina chatting with other boat people—Canadians, Americans, a few Brits and Mexicans. Nick was right: Many had come over from Key West and planned to return shortly.

On the fantail of a fifty-footer from Georgia a white-haired man was filleting fish. "Out early and in early before the wind kicked up."

"Good fishing?"

"Good as it gets. Marlin running. Grouper and yellow-tail for eating."

"Where to next?"

He pointed over his shoulder with his bloody knife. "Key West soon as the weather clears. Day after tomorrow maybe. I like it flat."

"Me too. But my captain's heading out tonight."

"I've seen twenty-foot seas in the Gulf Stream. What sort of boat?"

Con pointed across the marina. "That old cruiser."

The man shook his head. "Welcome to wait and come back with me. If it's calm Thursday I'm off at sunrise."

*

Back at the Pilar Nick stood astern staring out to sea. "Wind's picked up a few knots."

"Anyone going out?"

Nick shook his head. "Maybe it'll lay down later."

Con hung around, dozing in a deckchair, dipping into Dos Passos, drinking the occasional beer. The afternoon crept by. By sunset the wind had lessened, though he could still see whitecaps offshore. Nick was readying the Pilar for the trip back, but Con still didn't know if he was going along.

"Wait here, Conman." With that Nick leapt onto the dock and strode toward the customs shed.

Finally Con made a decision. Usually he had no plan, just hopping aboard whatever floated by. Which had gotten him this far. But that seemed far enough, he reasoned, acknowledging the prospect of hard time in Havana and the dubious nature of any Spanish treasure. He'd grab his five gees, cut his losses, and hitch back with the Georgian.

He went below and found his backpack. Into it he stuffed his rain jacket and shaving kit. He heard Nick's footfall on the deck and poked his head out the gangway. Nick said:

"Not tonight, Conman. A few boats tried and had to come back."

"What about Ricardo?"

Nick pulled a beer from the ice chest. "He'll figure it out sooner or later."

*

Next morning, another gray one, they again enlisted Marcos to guard the boat and took a taxi into Habana Vieja. At the Hotel Ambos Mundos, a ritzy joint catering to visiting politicos and businessmen, they breakfasted on eggs with hot sauce and guava cream-cheese pastries. At ten, when they stepped back onto the sidewalk, the sun was shining. Nick gazed at the eastern sky. "Looks good."

They walked to the Palacio Vienna Hotel and again mounted the gritty staircase. The place now seemed deserted. No children played at the precipice, no spies lurked in the hallway. Nick knocked at Aurora's door, which, they saw, had no padlocks on the outside. After a silent minute Nick knocked again. Through the door they heard shuffling footsteps then a voice: "¿Quién?"

"Soy yo, Nicholas."

"Minuto."

They waited a minute, two, three. The door opened and Aurora—dressed in blue jeans and silk turquoise blouse, the cowrie shells still strung around her neck—waved them in. She shut it behind them, apologizing. "Lo siento. I was still asleep. Siéntense."

They sat. She put the teakettle on the burner. Nick said: "Discúlpanos. Está temprano."

"Está bien. We were up late, Ricardo and I."

"¿Que pasó?"

She laid a hand on Con's shoulder and left it there. He felt it in his chest.

"We didn't know with the weather."

"My fault. Should have had a fallback plan."

"There was no other way. Ricardo swam out. I waited on shore. He clung to the channel marker two hours but saw no boats going out. So he swam back and returned to his barracks, and I came home by bus."

When the water was ready she poured out three cups. Nick squeezed a lime into his tea. "I know this is difficult, Aurora. To help your brother, your only family, leave you. Many thanks for your aid."

She nodded. "It is dangerous for him to stay."

"Once Ricardo is safe we'll devise a means for you to join him."

"Yo entiendo. Now only Ricardo matters."

"We will do it tonight. The weather looks fine."

Con nodded agreement even though he knew he wouldn't be going along.

Chapter Sixteen

No, it wasn't a dream, he told himself, seeing Aurora beside him in the backseat of the taxi, a Toyota van he'd hired for the day, as they motored west toward Pinar del Rio.

In her apartment that morning she had said, "Yesterday I promised to show you my island when you returned. Now you have returned."

They invited Nick along but he begged off. "Gracias, but I have seen your beautiful island. What's more, I need to prepare for a trip."

The warm wind blew through her black hair. They cruised down a largely deserted autobahn where, at cloverleaves, groups of travelers awaited buses. Others attempted to hitchhike on the underused highway, waving at their van as it passed.

Soon Aurora directed the driver onto a two-lane road where they wound past thatched-roofed farms, tobacco plantations, and stands of banana trees. Then low coffee trees, with orchids blooming along the roadside, the air smelling of flowers and spice.

They pulled to the side of the road at a crude barn. Inside they bought ripe mangos and ate them sitting on a rustic bench in the shade behind the structure. An earthy aroma reminiscent of burnt peanuts came to Con, a scent he associated with the tropics. Aurora reached over with a handkerchief to wipe mango juice from his chin.

"Tell me of your life in Key West."

Her question gave him pause. What of his life in Key West? In a flash he saw that he had again stepped off the Buddha's Noble Eightfold Path. The paving stone that always tripped him up was "right way of livelihood." He knew that these days he was more gigolo than writer and more bullshit-artist than artist.

"Mi vida es cómoda," he said, for it was about as easy a life as a man could want, perhaps too easy. "I visit my students, go to the beach, and read good books."

"¿Es todo?"

"Más o menos."

"'A strong man with no forethought is lazy,'" she said, as if quoting scripture.

"Some might say I'm lazy but I call it 'contemplative.'"

"But you write books as well, sí? Ricardo me dice que tú eres un novelista."

"Sí. I have published a novel."

"What now are you writing?"

He studied her intense blue eyes then looked up to the clear sky and the golden mangoes hanging in the tree before him. Her eyes were too innocent and expectant for him to disappoint her. He chewed his mango and thought.

"A book about a lonely americano," he said, "a decadent gringo who comes to Cuba and is touched by the simplicity of the hard lives here, the ongoing struggle of its people, and the love of a beautiful woman."

"¿Y entonces qué pasa? What does he do about it?"

Con turned back and gazed into her eyes. "I don't

know. I must write the next chapter."

*

The taxi snaked through the hills past green gorges, tobacco barns, and blue rivers. Here, away from Havana, the air came clear and fresh tasting. Then as they descended beside a river gorge he smelled the sea.

They entered a dusty seaside town, the buildings there also in disrepair. Men idled in the town square. The taxi stopped. Aurora told the driver when to meet them in the *zócalo*, and Con gave him money for his afternoon meal.

She led Con down a shaded lane to a once grand *finca*, plaster and paint peeling, on a shore where blue waves lapped. In back on a palm-shaded patio two couples speaking French sat at one of three plastic tables. A white-haired man carrying a tray appeared from the house to greet them. As they sat, he gave them hand-printed menus and disappeared back into the house.

"Éste es típico," Aurora explained. "Un paladar. Not strictly permitted but not forbidden. Families sell meals to tourists to earn a few dollars or euros. Otherwise one must make due on twenty dollars a month, más o menos."

"How can you buy a beer or a new dress?"

"One has to be clever."

"There seems to be few joys."

"I have my music. I am privileged to live as an artist with the support of the people. And I have the comforts of my faith."

"¿Eres tú católico?"

She studied him for a moment. He became conscious of the sound of waves slapping the rocks. Finally she said: "My mother was Catholic and taught me about the saints. Now I follow the way of the saints."

A pine warbler sang from a nearby mangrove and he looked up. Bougainvillea wandered magenta and peach-colored atop a trellis. Silver palms crouched beneath taller coconut palms. *Azucenas, geranios,* and other potted plants flowered nearby. She followed his gaze and said:

"This is what I long for most: the palm trees, the lilies, the geraniums. To have soil between my toes."

The white-haired man returned, and they ordered beer and grilled snapper. When he left she asked Con: "What do you read?"

He began listing his favorites: Twain, Hemingway, Cather; Maupassant, Simenon, Turgenev…

"Sí, sí," she interrupted. "But they are dead. Who is alive and writing? Here it is difficult to know anything."

The fish when it came was delicious but accompanied by bland cole slaw and canned peas. Afterward they sat sipping rum and staring out over the water. The French-speaking couples had left.

She asked: "¿Conoces España?"

"I know Barcelona and Majorca. Both very beautiful."

"I want to see Madrid and to hear the music and to sing there."

"You are ambitious."

She nodded. "I want to sing the songs I write. At the Casa de Tango I sing only approved songs. On his birthday I am required to sing to El Líder. And once a year I give a recital, next month. Will you come?"

A breeze blew Aurora's curling black hair across her cheek and carried to him the scents of sea and perfume. A gull came up the shore to beg. He shooed him away.

"Tal vez. But it is not easy. There are no flights. And it is possible to lose your passport for traveling here."

"Sí, es difícil. Even to communicate. Letters never arrive, packages confiscated. Only ninety miles apart but we live in two worlds." She looked out to sea, squinting as if trying to glimpse the American shore there. "And Ricardo is leaving for the other one."

"Why are you not going with him?"

She folded her hands in her lap. "The long swim is dangerous, Ricardo says, and there is only room for one. Besides, it is difficult to live in America without work even with the stipend for refugees. He will have work with Señor Nicholas on the sea and I would be alone. But for me, without speaking English....As a child I was taught only Russian. He will send for me later. At least here I am able to sing."

*

They walked down a beach dotted with palms and mangroves, carrying their sandals, the water warm on his ankles. As he studied her, the dreamlike feeling returned. Her turquoise blouse matched the sea, which seemed to whisper to him as benign waves came to shore and retreated, as it were breathing.

"Aurora, sing for me. Sing me one of your songs."

She stopped, turned, and looked up and down the beach. Then pressing her hands together she began to sing with clear, piercing voice. She sang of birds, of the beautiful songbirds of the Americas that visited Cuba on their way north and south in spring and fall but did not stay. He listened, watching her lips. When she finished she dropped her head.

"¡Qué bella!" he said. "Gracias, Aurora."

Down the beach another hundred yards at a deserted cove she threw her shoes on the sand and began to unbutton her blouse.

"Ven, Constantino. Let's swim."

He pulled off his jeans, watching her wade naked into the sea: square-shouldered, small-waisted, brown-skinned. What he had perceived earlier as Spanish features—the large eyes, straight, flaring nose, and brown skin—now struck him as African. She disappeared into the water and he followed.

They swam out a hundred yards. Then she turned and came to him. Treading water she lifted the cowrie-shell necklace over her head and placed it around his neck.

"This will guard you and bring you luck on your trip back and on all your journeys. As long as your heart is pure you will be protected, praise the saints. And tonight I will make a sacrifice to please the orishas."

"Ah! The way of the saints: Santería. Are you a priestess?"

"'The creator has made us with different qualities.'... Sí, soy santera but we do not speak of this."

She pulled herself to him and he felt his heart quicken as her breasts brushed his chest.

"I know, Constantino, that once we part we may never see each other again. So kiss me before you go."

Chapter Seventeen

The sun was setting by the time he returned to the Pilar. It had been an odd, dreamlike day, and Con felt decidedly odd, as if he had been inhabited by another soul.

Nick sat on the fantail, smoking. "Figured I'd see you before I take off. Guess you want your dough."

Con pulled a beer from the ice chest. "Later's fine."

He spied the rum bottle on the fantail next to Nick and poured himself a double.

"I've been going over the pros and cons all day, Nick. The rational approach dictates caution. To do the safe thing, the sure thing." He threw back the rum. "But I got some good advice recently: Be bold and follow your heart. I've never trusted the rational approach anyway. Every time I do I fuck up royally and afterward feel like hell for not being myself. So count me in."

Nick puffed on his pipe. "Good. I can use you. Just don't get so potted that I have to pull you both from the water."

"Just one boilermaker for ballast."

They stowed the rum and other gear and readied the Pilar. Finally they carried the ice chest below and positioned it on the floor in the nose, pressed against the compartment where the stolen charts and machine gun lay.

*

When it was dark, Nick started the engine. Con stepped onto the dock to cast off the stern line, and the Pilar swung around. He loosened the bowline from the cleat and jumped on board.

Nary a breath of wind, the marina waters looking like black glass. With no moon he couldn't tell about the open sea but figured it was okay. Nick stood silent at the helm as they slid past the lights of other boats moored there.

At the customs shed Con leapt onto the dock and tied up. From the concrete-block building stepped not Javier or Rafael but a thin officer with Vaselined hair who looked like a seagull caught in an oil slick. Nick invited him on board. Without speaking he moved onto the deck. Nick asked:

"¿Quisiera usted un apertivo o cervezita?"

He refused the drink offer with a shake of his head and opened the engine hold, shining a flashlight into it.

"We were having a little trouble with it coming across," said Nick. "If she starts running rough again I may have to stop beyond the channel and work on the carburetor."

The man made no response. Closing the hatch he asked: "What did you purchase in Cuba?"

Nick spread his hands. "Nada. Solamente la comida y cerveza."

The man descended the few steps into the cabin and disappeared. Nick went to the helm to study the chart there. But Con could tell it was just an act and sat on the engine cover trying to look unconcerned. Then they heard the ice chest scraping across the cabin floor. He saw Nick's square frame freeze.

Long minutes passed. Con felt his stomach churn and blood pulsing in his neck. He stared at Nick. He knew Nick could feel his eyes on him, but he avoided eye contact. Then they heard footsteps and turned toward the gangway.

The man's head appeared. He climbed the steps one by one. At the top he faced Nick. "Buen viaje, Capitán. I hope you return soon." He extended his hand: "Me llamo Jaime."

Nick shook it. "Mucho gusto, Jaime."

The engine coughed as they powered away from the dock.

"Time for another boilermaker," Nick said. "And make mine a double."

Beyond the marina the sea lay dark and flat with but a light chop. The Pilar chugged along as if in no hurry. Nick threw back his rum and took a pull on his beer. "A little adventure gets the blood moving, eh, Conman?"

"To the contrary: Stops heart."

But he saw Nick was right. He'd not felt so alive since Cat shot at him. Yes, writers went through hell but it was a hell of their own making, and when day was done you'd run no greater risk than possibly catching a hangnail on a shift key. But this was different. The risk was real and so was the emotion.

They were doing five knots. Still it took but a few minutes before the last channel marker came into sight a half mile off shore. As they approached it Nick throttled down. They glided toward it in the dark, waves sucking at the side of the boat. Nick gazed back at the lights of the marina then ahead for signs of other boats.

Con moved onto the fantail and flopped the hinged ladder down into the sea. The red-painted channel marker slid toward him. Then he saw a dark shape clinging there, watched it move toward the ladder, and spied Ricardo's head coming out of the black water. Con reached out a hand, and next the Cuban was climbing up the ladder in a dripping black wetsuit.

Nick glanced back to see Ricardo climbing aboard. "Get the ladder up!"

"Wait!" Con called.

He knelt and extended his hand toward a second black shape swimming from the marker. Hair clinging to her face, Aurora emerged and struggled up the ladder and onto the deck. Nick saw her and fixed his gaze on Con.

"Okay, Conman. Give them some dry clothes, stow them with the charts if they'll fit, and make sure there's no water on the cabin floor. Tie their wetsuits round the old anchor on the fantail. If anyone comes close push it in." With that Nick moved the Pilar off into the dark.

It took some doing but Con managed to cram Aurora and Ricardo back to front, like spoons, into the compartment, with her grasping the charts and machine gun between her breasts, just as he'd envisioned. She smiled. He put the panel back in place and screwed it down.

Back on deck he retrieved from storage the old anchor, the one he'd found off Sand Key, carried it aft and tied the wetsuits around it. Next he placed it on the fantail beside the telescoped ladder where he could push it off with his foot if the Cuban Coast Guard got curious. Finally he went to the bridge and stood beside Nick.

"Everything stowed?"

"Todo."

Nick's eyes searched the black horizon. He drained off his beer and wiped his lips with the back of his hand. "Guess it's no worse smuggling two refugees than one."

"That was my take."

"You might have said something."

"Rather beg forgiveness rather than ask permission. I tried to follow The Code but some of this stuff ain't in there."

"Women take up an entire chapter written in invisible ink."

"This one's double trouble, maybe triple. Beautiful, soulful, talented, and thus hard to shake."

"You'll find a way."

"Likely won't have to. She said I shouldn't feel responsible for her. That by taking her along I'd be doing her a great service she'd be forever grateful for. That we could go our separate ways and her fate wasn't my lookout."

Nick nodded. "All the right things. Smart girl. But Ricardo would have sent for her eventually."

"That's dicey."

"So is this."

"She seemed desperate to come now. Said next year would be too late."

He saw Nick's eyes tighten. His gaze had fixed on the lights of a fast-approaching ship. They stood rigid. Finally Nick said: "Yep. Coast Guard. Better saunter back and tip the wetsuits over."

Con strolled aft and grabbed the back of the bimini with both hands, as if gazing wistfully at the lights of Havana, such as they were. But his heart was racing. After a moment he pushed the wetsuits and anchor off the fantail with his foot. When he returned to the bridge Nick said: "Fucker's taking a good look."

The Coast Guard gunboat, a fifty-footer, passed portside at thirty yards. Nick waved and gave a thumbs up. "Maybe Jaime asked them to check on us to see if we'd fixed our carburetor."

"Good old Jaime."

"Most folks are better than their governments."

"That's not saying much."

The Cuban ship turned and motored off into the dark. Nick pushed the throttle forward.

After an hour, as they cut across the inky sea, Nick said

to him: "Fetch us a couple Cristales from the ice chest, Conman. We'll drink to leaving Cuban waters. And you can get your girlfriend out too."

*

A warm night. Nick stood at the wheel as the Pilar rocked through the Gulf Stream. Ricardo slept in the hammock, which swayed with each lurch of the boat over four-foot swells. On the banquette Aurora, dressed in one of Nick's khaki shirts, lay curled, orange life vest under her head, dead to the world. Con sat on the deck aft, leaning against the fantail, feeling the vibration of the engine through the boards.

He dozed in and out, thinking on what would happen when he returned to Key West. Although the money from Nick would pay his back taxes, turn on the lights, and square the rent with Berman, he knew it was but a temporary fix. And no fix at all for what he'd been wrestling with most: his writer's block. But he wondered if he hadn't subdued that as well, or at least gained a hammerlock on it. Maybe the plot he had recited extemporaneously to Aurora would ferment and gather strength.

He dozed off again and when he woke Con sensed that the vibration had ceased. He looked up to see that Nick had lifted the engine hatch and was peering into the hold with a flashlight. Con pushed up from the deck and moved next to him. "What's up?"

"Front gas tank ran dry so I switched to the second. When I tried restarting her, nothing."

"Where are we?"

"In the middle of the Florida Straits." Nick lifted his chin aft. "Havana's twenty-five miles thataway, Key West sixty-five the other. Current would carry us to Key Largo eventually."

"'Eventually'?"

"Two or three days given good weather."

As if on cue, lightning lit up the southeast horizon. Then another flash.

"Good material, Conman."

"If we live through it."

"That's no joke. Folks disappear out here. They buy a yacht and sail up the coast staying in sight of land then are never heard from again. Trouble is, Junior never even added a can of oil to his car. If you plan to have a relationship with machinery, especially the kind that can founder in twenty-foot seas, you'd better be willing to get your hands dirty and eat, sleep, and breathe with it. If you haven't done your homework all the charisma in the world won't keep you afloat. Not like politics and business and such where bullshit and money will keep you going even if you don't have a clue. Might be a good thing if mistakes were fatal in all endeavors: weed out the amateurs and loudmouths. As it stands the phonies rule except when it's time to ride out a gale or land a plane in the dark."

Con went below to grab a beer. When he came back up Nick was wiping his hands on a towel. "Just a loose starter wire. Go up and try her."

At the helm Con turned the key. The starter ground and the V-8 began rumbling. Nick closed the hatch. "Head her north-northwest, Conman," he said and went below.

Con manned the wheel, drinking it all in. The Pilar was mowing down the waves. He rocked back grasping the wheel as she climbed each swell and leaned into it as the vessel slid down the other side. Behind him their human contraband slept and, above, the black sky was linted with silver stars. The wind blew through his hair and the mingling smells of sea and gasoline enfolded him.

Soon Nick came back up with two mojitos, handed him one, and raised the other. "To the freedom of the open seas."

"To freedom."

They clinked glasses together. Con stared out at the obscure horizon, where he perceived the first feeble signs of dawn.

"I have all the freedom in the world but when I'm not writing it's like I'm in prison. But now…I told Aurora I was writing a book, and I think maybe I am. It came to me when she asked me what I was working on—sprang out if not fully formed at least taking shape: A story about a guy who…"

Nick held up a hand to stop him. "Never talk about your work when you're working. Bad luck. Takes the magic dust off the butterfly's wings and it can't get off the ground. And a writer's always working even when it looks like he's just fucking-off or sleeping. If I start talking about it then I'm jiggering my story, concretizing it when I still want it pliable.

"Guard these like your cojones, Conman: your material, your originality, your independence, and your integrity. When they tell you the bell tolls for thee and mean you better join in or be left out in the cold, don't listen to the bastids. Don't join in and don't bitch yourself by being false to your work or to who you are. Don't be a talker, be a listener: Be a writer. That's where I bitched myself, when I stopped being sensitive and honest to myself and started acting like Hemingway the Writer and became that persona and couldn't keep my mouth shut and surrounded myself with sycophants who let me go on with the masquerade. Like I told the folks in Sweden, the writer grows in public stature as he sheds his loneliness, and often his work deteriorates. At a certain point fools take over and no one complains. And Keats, don't forget Keats."

"The beauty truth, truth beauty bit?"

"And always remember that the only failure is quitting. We each owe God a death and you can go as a quitter or as a glorious Quixote who was true to one good thing. And the bad taste of years of struggling would be just one big gob of spit."

Con saw Nick bite his bottom lip, as if it to keep it from trembling. Hemingway a quitter? Maybe Nick saw it that way, but Con saw it differently. Hem's mind and his talent and his material quit him, not the other way around.

Nick went on as if again reading Con's mind: "It's a strange sort of Paradise I've landed in where a man can't do the one thing that always gave him the most pleasure. That's why you have to do it now, Conman, or never. For me it comes by helping you. Lets me keep my hand in. If I succeed they let me write you a letter. When you get that, you'll know you've done it."

Nick shook his head as if to dispel cobwebs there. "Here, take the wheel. Methinks I've lost an oar, Aeneas, and am turning in circles. Thus spake many a wandering soul."

With that Nick went to the stern, poured himself a rum, and stood staring at the black sea.

PART THREE: HURRICANE

Chapter Eighteen

Con's return to Key West came with a certain melancholia despite the seed for the new book growing within him. Maybe it was the anxiety that came with it, for he was already acquainted with the pains of gestation and birth he would likely face over the next months and perhaps years as his book took shape, grew and was born. But there was also the question of being honest in his writing, not being a phony or kidding himself. Easier said than done. As Hemingway once noted, "The most essential gift for a good writer is a built-in, shockproof shit detector. This is the writer's radar and all great writers have it." Con wondered if he still did.

On a flat, sunny day he powered out to Sand Key with Johannsen aboard Tailchaser. After a half an hour in the water Johannsen returned to the boat but Con continued on, enchanted as always by the surreal colors of the underwater world. The water felt warm, near ninety, and lay crystal clear on the reef that day.

He snorkeled up between two fingers of coral where the water grew shallower, following a school of iridescent blue tang. The fish he tailed undulated over yellow-gold coral as sun rays lit them cobalt and royal. Then ahead he saw a dark shape disappear behind a coral stand and thought: nurse shark, which while big and dark was passive and harmless. Con was curious, but the water grew shallower there and he didn't want to brush up against the coral. So he turned and swam back toward the boat. It was then he noticed Johannsen standing astern Tailchaser holding a beer in one hand and waving with the other. He took a sip and called:

"Check behind you."

Looking over his shoulder Con spied some twenty yards distant the black dorsal fin of a bull shark cutting through the water toward him. Adrenaline hurrying his heart, he thrashed toward the boat, flew up the ladder in his dive fins, and splayed on the rear platform gasping.

Johannsen guffawed. "You flopped on the fantail like a flying fish."

"You can laugh," Con said pulling off his fins. "Your ass was safely aboard."

Johannsen sucked on his beer. "Wonder why he didn't go for yours? He was right there. Maybe it's the talisman the Cuban broad gave you."

Con pulled a beer from the cooler and touched the cowrie shells strung around his neck. "Could be."

Johannsen shook his head. "Simpleminded pagan."

They drank down their beers and opened two more as they lazed on the cushioned bow. Con gazed at the Mule Keys across water that lay as still as a pond's as the sun seared him.

"Never seen it so flat."

"It's the hurricane."

"What hurricane?"

"Hector, coming to hector us. Should be here within days. You were lucky to get out of Cuba when you did."

"In more ways than one."

"How'd you duck the Feds?"

"Bustamante was waiting on Stock Island. Aurora and her brother jumped off the boat and into his cab before we called Customs. They lay low for a few days then surrendered to the first cop they saw. Claimed to have swum ashore when their boat sank and asked for asylum. But I haven't seen her since."

"What about Eva?"

"Soon as she saw my light on she called to ask if the coast was clear."

"Still pressing for marriage?"

"Full-court."

"You get the five gees from Nick?"

Con nodded as he brought the beer bottle to his lips. "Most went to square accounts."

"Any students left?"

"Yeah, but the hurricane could scatter them. Be hard even to cover my bar tabs."

"Some would pay the rent first."

"I can't live like an accountant."

"But as a no-count."

"Easy for you to say after fucking yourself into millions."

"She got good value. By the way, Wild Cat still stalking you?"

"Haven't seen her. Though I did find ten emails from her when I got the juice turned back on."

Johannsen studied him. "She loves you and wants to spend her life with you, not just two years. A significant desire. Least you could do is respond in some honest way."

"Flight is an honest response. She's too high-strung and high-maintenance. She'd make my life hell."

"Or heaven if you could tame her."

"Cat's the least of my worries. I need some new students. But it's hurricane season not tourist season. Snowbirds won't fly south for another four months."

"You could get a job."

Con shook his head. "Just started a new book."

"Eva's offer's looking better and better."

"Something will turn up."

"Unfortunately it's Hurricane Hector. You're welcome to board up and board with Nadya and me. I've got a ten-kilowatt generator, a freezer full of fish, and a fridge full of beer."

"There's a country song in there somewhere."

*

Con woke late and checked the National Weather Service channel, where a robotic voice gave the temperature and went on to say that it would be fair that day in the Florida Keys despite Hurricane Hector lurking in the Atlantic. The local TV newscast began with a colorful storm-track cornucopia suggesting where Hector might dump his dubious fruits. If he approached the Keys, hardware stores would advertise specials on plywood sheets to board up windows against projectiles, trucks loaded with jugs of spring water would back up to supermarket loading docks, and lines would form at gasoline pumps in anticipation of possible single-file flight up U.S. 1 in cars packed with kids, pets, and family photo-albums. Then, as in most cases, when the storm veered south to Cuba or north to the Carolinas, the Conchs would be stuck with stacks of rotting plywood in the backyard and a sense of ennui. Though on occasion a storm like Georges or Wilma would charge through the Florida Straits or sneak through the back door off the Gulf and cause significant damage and disruption.

Con knew that if Hector did strike Key West, he'd be stuck inside for days and afterward the sea would be opaque for weeks. Today might be his last chance to snorkel for a month.

He dialed Eva's cell phone but got no answer. So he walked the few blocks over to her place—an old Conch house cut up into apartments—and up the back stairs. When he knocked, an unshaven man in a white wife-beater answered the door. Another man with tattoos on his neck sat at a Formica table smoking a cigarette.

"Eva here?"

The smoker stared at Con. The other motioned with his head.

Con walked through the tobacco-scented kitchen, moved down the unswept hall, and banged on a closed bedroom door where he noticed hardware for a padlock, which made him think of Aurora's Havana apartment. Through the door he heard Eva say something in Czech, presumably.

"It's me, Con."

He heard her fumbling with the lock. After a few seconds she opened the door a crack, saw it was really him, and let him slide through. As she closed the door behind him he spied additional hardware on the jamb there.

"When I go away I lock from outside," she explained. "When I am home I lock from inside." Seeing the concern on his face she added: "Is nothing really. One time Vladimir came home drunk and opened my door by mistake."

On the worn wood floor sat a lamp and a mattress. No dresser, no desk, no chair. Her clothes rested in cardboard boxes along the wall. He looked at Eva trying to gauge what it was like inside her skin, realizing how their time together—safe, carefree, pleasurable—must contrast with her gritty daily grind.

"Come on, Baby, let's hit the beach—Bahia Honda if I can get Johannsen's car. You free?"

Eva spread her arms. "For you free. Everyone else pays."

She grabbed her swimsuit and towel, and together they fled her dungeon.

*

Back at his place Con raised Johannsen on his cell phone. In the background he heard the sound of wind and sea and Nadya spouting something in Russian and laughing.

"I trust you're enjoying yourself, Jojo."

"You bet I am."

Johannsen directed him to the spare house-key hidden in the fountain and the Porsche key in the pantry. Downstairs Eva fired up her motor scooter and Con hopped on back. At Johannsen's house they traded the Yamaha for the Johannsen's 1996 polar-silver Porsche 911 Cabriolet—bought by his ex as a wedding gift—and headed up U.S. 1 with the top down.

Con saw that, yeah, he was damn near destitute, Eva was selling herself just to live in a hovel with leering bohunks, and Hurricane Hector was poised to kick their butts, but who gave a fuck, really? Buddha said to live in the moment and the moment was just fine: blue skies, shimmering waters, the purring German machine, and the Czech tart with bleached hair streaming out behind her in the wind.

They stopped on Big Pine Key for take-out sandwiches and beer. At Bahia Honda State Park the Atlantic lay a placid blue beyond the long, white-sand beach. Behind the dunes silver palms whistled in a light wind and salty aromas of sea and damp sand rode with it. Eva and Con spread their towels on the hot beach.

With their snorkels they swam out a hundred yards, where the water was still not over his head. The sculptured sand bottom gave way to sea grass where shiners and other small fish played, conchs lazed, and spiny lobsters lurked beneath sponges. A high midday sun lit the underwater world in glistening greens and grays. Eva swam on ahead in her faux-leopard bikini, looking like Sheena as she sliced to the bottom to investigate a stone crab.

Back on the beach they lounged on their towels and lunched on fried grouper with canned beer.

"Tell me, Eva: Why do you live with people you can't trust?"

"Is temporary."

"Is dangerous. You're making good money. Find a place with better roommates. Another woman maybe."

"I lived with Lela for two weeks but that was more dangerous. Men came at all hours and tried to get sex from me for money like from Lela."

"You still could afford better."

"I am saving money. Soon I will have three thousand for down payment on marriage. Then I quit sexy job and work as waitress to pay rent and buy you vodka."

Eva sat on her white Hilton beach towel, bent knees together, near-platinum hair drying spread on her bronzed back, the scent of coconut oil rising from her smooth skin. He knew that, for all her seeming carefree ways and composure, she surely felt vulnerable and was fighting to find her way in the world and praying that he would help her. He fought off an urge to take her in his arms and accept her marriage proposal on the spot. Con still harbored the belief—perhaps irrationally—that something would turn up, that he'd find his own Atocha, whatever form it might take.

"I'm thinking about it, Eva. A very seductive offer."

"I will be seductive every day."

"I know you would," he said, thinking, not bad: seduced daily and getting paid for it. Well, bought and paid. Coupled with cohabitation, the prospect of being a kept man and hubby made him itchy. He recalled the blissless days with Francesca: her mood swings from sullen to fiery, the running conversation that lasted five years, the pointless arguments. However, he'd observed that support was always an attendance prize: No one ever just put the check in the mail.

Also, though within the seeming letter of the law the marriage involved a deception, even if it was only the government being deceived and its immigration laws being circumvented. Still, it reminded him of his earlier capitulation to his agent to get his book published, going against his heart to get the money and all that went with it. Ambition had ruled the day and ultimately bitched him and his work. He recalled Nick's admonition to guard his material, originality, independence, and integrity, and saw he would be sacrificing the last two in Eva's marital scheme. Con felt Nick looking over his shoulder disapprovingly—a sensation so strong that he fought an urge to check the dunes behind him.

Eva grabbed his arm and stared over his shoulder, eyes wide. "Look, Cone!" He turned. "Cyclone!"

A waterspout on the Gulfside was heading their way. Scary looking to an inlander wary of tornadoes but, he assured Eva, relatively harmless. Soon it crossed over the narrow strip of key to the east and dissipated in the Atlantic. Then, magically, a rainbow appeared in its place.

An omen, Con thought. Perhaps the whirlwind he felt swirling in his own life would dissolve into a figurative rainbow with the promised pot of gold—literal or otherwise—at its end. He got a sudden vision of Nick as his savior, the agent of his deliverance. An absurd, unreasonable feeling, he knew, but a heartfelt one.

Although Nick had mentioned nothing more about the Atocha and the treasure maps, he had come up with the promised five thousand bucks and helped Con get thinking about a new book in the process. Perhaps Nick would bring him more good luck and needed aid. Even the real Hemingway had Ezra, Gertrude, Ford, and Sherwood giving him guidance when he needed it. Even writing coaches needed writing coaches. Writers should work alone, as Nick had said, but you can't do it alone.

Con looked around for some wood to knock on to assure his treasure, but all he found was sand and seashells.

Chapter Nineteen

That night Con tried to read himself to sleep, lying abed with one of Simenon's mysteries, which usually gave him good dreams of Paris. But his thoughts kept straying to his incipient story set in Cuba and to the Santeria priestess—a goddess, perhaps—who works some black magic on behalf of his autobiographic protagonist. So he got up and went to his desk and turned on his laptop.

He sat staring at the glowing screen but not seeing it. Instead he saw himself in Cuba, saw Aurora wading naked into the sea, and felt his heart quicken. Con sensed a hint of disturbed air on the back of his neck, enough to make him look up. A scent of sweet pipe tobacco came to mind and with it an image of Nick, who spoke to him.

"Make me feel it, Conman. Make it happen to me too so it becomes my experience as well and part of my life. Not an easy thing to do but that's the job."

So he wrote down watching her move naked into the sea and wrote down the things that produced the emotion in him: the sheen of her skin, the shape of her hips, the feel of warm water on his legs and then, when he approached her, the papaya scent of her and the electricity of her legs against his in the water.

"He sensed her breasts pressing against him," Con wrote, "her breath on his lips, her words coming to him with weight, as if palpable. 'Besame antes de salir…Kiss me well before you go, Martín, before they take you away…'"

His cell phone buzzed on his desk. He looked down at the number but didn't recognize it. Wrong number, he figured, but picked it up just to stop it and deter another interruption. But then he heard Eva's voice issue from it:

"Cone, I have a job for you. You make two hundred dollars easy. The night manager is too drunk."

"The night manager where?"

"Here, at Key West Spa."

Which was no spa at all, he knew, but a faux brothel near the south end of Duval Street, where a guy could get fucked but only figuratively. Out of curiosity Johannsen had led him there one drunken night. Inside they found a disinterested blonde who wanted a hundred dollars just to disrobe, something you could get for free from ten dancers at any strip joint. He now understood why Eva had been vague about where she worked.

*

Con pedaled his bike through dark streets still warm that smelled of jasmine and dead fish. He soon pushed through the front door of the single-story white-frame bungalow. There he was confronted by a tall, tawdry brunette in red corset and high heels.

"You want a special dance with Lela?" she asked, twisting his nipple through his tee shirt.

"Free sample?"

"You are joking."

"I'm looking for Eva."

"She is with a customer."

"I'll wait."

He planted himself on a leatherette sofa in the front room, which smelled of pine-scent room-deodorizer. After a few minutes Eva appeared with her purse, donning a sweater. As he rose she lay a hand on his forearm.

"I would do it, Cone, but I can't keep my eyes open."

She showed him the ropes, which consisted of greeting customers, fixing them up with the women in the back rooms, and then spying on them through a peephole to make sure nothing illegal, like actual sex, occurred. Which he figured made for some disgruntled customers. But she said nothing about that.

Eva kissed him goodbye, and he moved behind the counter. Con looked from the sordid couch to the cheap ceiling fan to the security camera aimed down at him, and his thoughts went back to the santera in the sea.

*

Fifteen minutes later his first customers arrived, an attractive couple, nicely dressed and tipsy.

"On your honeymoon?" he asked.

The man held up two fingers. "Second." The woman held up three fingers.

Con introduced them to Lela, ran the guy's credit card, and read them the house rules. Off they went. After a few minutes he strolled back to Lela's door and peered through the fisheye peephole.

Naked except for her red shoes, Lela stood beside a sofa in front of which the husband, also naked, knelt performing cunnilingus on his wife. Soon the couple traded places and the wife reciprocated. Next the woman lay on the sofa, guided her husband into her, and beckoned to Lela. "I want to lick you," Con heard the woman say through the door.

At this point, according to his job description, he should have interrupted their activity to keep the establishment legally compliant. Instead Con watched, noting surreptitious glances by both husband and wife toward the door where he stood, and he realized he was part of it, that they thrilled at being watched. He turned away.

After the couple left, Lela took Con to a corner out of the gaze of the overhead camera and, with a licentious wink, handed him a twenty-dollar bill.

He pocketed the money. "America's a beautiful country, no?"

Lela shrugged.

Over the next hours four male customers appeared at intervals. Con performed the routine of introductions, ground rules recitation and cash or credit-card payment. He no longer bothered peering through the peepholes, instead reading old copies of *Cosmopolitan* he found in the desk.

He dozed. Then he was awakened by the sound of a door slamming. A burly customer with a New Jersey accent came from the back zipping up his pants.

"Two hundred bucks and she won't even touch it. What the fuck kind of whorehouse is this?"

Con spread his hands. "You knew the rules."

The man moved toward him, clenching his fists. "I want my fucking money back."

Con looked from him to the surveillance camera and back again. He flicked his eyes first toward the camera then toward the front door. The man followed him outside and stood huffing on the sidewalk.

Con raised his palms. "Look. I'm just filling in tonight and agree it's a racket. Give me a credit card and I'll give you back your two cee-notes. Then you call MasterCard and dispute it."

Placated, the man soon left with his cash.

Con got a cigarette from Lela and sat on the front steps smoking. It was a lovely, starlit night. He thought of Eva, now asleep behind her padlocked door. He imagined her with the man from New Jersey, stripping for him, fondling herself, perhaps more. He replayed in his mind her joy in snorkeling, her ready laugh and high spirits, and her professed love for him. Johannsen had counseled him on his need to respond to the love of a woman. He saw he had not yet properly done so with neither Eva nor Cat.

And what of his muse? Most likely the goddess Calliope, with her writing tablet, who had inspired Homer to write both the *Iliad* and the *Odyssey*. Assuming she bore some love for him, Con Martens, as well, how best to respond? He knew the answer. There was but one way: to submit to his work as if a sacred calling, to subjugate his ego and let Her speak through him. To become a mere vessel from which would issue a holy libation, divinely inspired.

At that instant he glanced up to see a shooting star flame and die in the southern sky, plummeting perhaps to Cuban shores. He heard Nick's voice: "All you have to do is write one true sentence. Write the truest sentence you know." He turned to see if Nick had somehow snuck up behind him, but there was no one.

Con threw his cigarette butt into the gutter and went back inside.

Chapter Twenty

Con woke to a breezy, rainy morning—the early outer bands of Hurricane Hector. He checked the storm's likely path on the National Weather Service website: one computer model had it veering south into the Gulf of Mexico, another had it deflecting north to Miami, and yet another had it heading for a direct hit on Key West.

But there was no use worrying about it. Out of his hands. Instead, recalling Nick's admonition about discipline, he went back to work on his novel. He sat on the verandah with his journal, sketching out a timeline of scenes he knew he wanted in it to get the chronology and causality right, working from the back to the front of the book. But it was hard not to be distracted by passing motor scooters, trash trucks, and the hourly Conch Tour Trolley, packed with tourists off cruise ships. From the faux, rubber-tire, open-air streetcar they stared up at him through the palms. Dressed in yellow-plastic rain-ponchos, the vacationers no doubt envied his privileged life of leisure, he figured. But of course they had no way of knowing he was but a step away from homelessness.

The red trolley turned the corner past the library, the driver's voice blaring from loudspeakers: "On your left note the splendidly restored Conch house of the famed Broadway producer…" Such drivel likely contributed to a surreal comprehension of Key West, Con reasoned, explaining in part why tourists routinely disobeyed traffic signals and did lines of cocaine off bar tops: "Hey, it's Key West, not real life!"

Again he got back to work but instead started thinking about the books he had been helping his students write: Marta's *Unsafe Sex*, Sandra's kiss-and-tell memoir, Rebecca Hemingway's celebrity-kin confession, and Cat's migratory farm-worker murder mystery. He realized that their books siphoned off energy for his own work. But his writing coaching paid his bills, at times, and built, he sensed, good karma that would bolster his new novel. Hoping to draw on that karma, he got back to work. Then from the street below he heard a woman's voice singing:

"Put a little love in your heart…"

He rose from his chair, peered over the rail, and spied the Picasso Lady, as the cops called her. For she was angular and square-faced and layered on her makeup in Cubist fashion, as if with a painter's knife. She stood before the library in the rain like a ghost junkie from Woodstock, singing hits of the 60s and 70s from a songbook she likely found in the trash. She followed with "All We Need Is Love" and "Blowing in the Wind." Impossible to write realistic fiction, Con mused, with all this madness going on around you. But she finally moved on and Con returned to his work.

A half hour had passed when he heard a car's engine idling below, two toots on the horn, and a raspy voice calling: "Hey! Conman!"

He looked over the rail again to see Nick's head sticking out the window of a pink taxi, its windshield wipers clicking like a metronome. Nick bellowed up to him: "Drop your cock and grab your slicker."

His words came as an order, not a debate parry. So Con put aside his pen, donned his rain jacket, and moved downstairs. When he closed the downstairs door behind him and stepped out on the sidewalk, he found a man in silk, palm-tree-covered shirt, pressed white slacks, and expensive loafers. He held an umbrella, sucked a cigar, and eyed the address over the door. He then looked at Con and said:

"You must be Constantine Martens."

Caught off guard and thinking the man an admiring reader, Con nodded. The man handed him an envelope.

"You've just been duly served a subpoena by an officer of the Missouri 22nd Judicial Circuit Court. Have a nice day."

The man turned and sauntered off down the block. An attorney on vacation, Con assumed, just having a little lawyerly fun.

Con slipped into the back seat behind Nick. At the steering wheel sat Bustamante. Con tore open the envelope, scanned the subpoena, and laughed.

"Good news?" asked Nick.

"Greetings from the State of Missouri, which seeks my presence in court next month to explain why I shouldn't pay four-thousand-two-hundred-fifty dollars and ninety cents in back taxes. 'Failure to appear could result in stiff penalties and an arrest warrant being issued.' No indication what they'd do if I show up penniless." He handed Nick the subpoena "Can't believe they found me. No forwarding address, no public record in Key West, no phone book listing."

Bustamante eyed Con in the rearview mirror as he moved the cab from the curb. "You got computer? That's how."

Nick looked up from the subpoena. "How's that?" he said in rhythm with the wipers.

Con answered: "They know what medicines and magazines you use, the size of your bar tabs, and whether you bet the ponies online. When I got behind on my credit-cards, I started getting email solicitations for tranquilizers. Bustamante's right."

"Then Orwell was on point about Big Brother."

"Big Mother's more like it," said Con, "trying to correct and 'sivilize' us, like Huck's Widow Douglas. But in this case she's not after your soul just your pocketbook, though may take along the other as collateral damage."

Nick licked his lips. "Gives me the willies. Boosty, steer us to a dry venue with dry gin."

*

At a strip-mall on the north side of town they entered a cavernous, smoky saloon smelling of beer, with jukebox rock blaring from overhead speakers. In the back room Con found Johannsen shooting pool and drinking vodka with Nadya, a tall Russian with close-set eyes. Her red hair seemed on fire, her face flushed. Nick ordered up a round of gin-and-tonics. Johannsen, who had taught capitalism in Moscow after communism tanked, turned to Nadya and started speaking Russian—a great knack, Con saw, in a town where half the strippers were ex-Warsaw-Pact chicks.

Hector's progress was being chronicled via The Weather Channel on a score of TVs hanging from the ceiling about the room, with a mix of sports shows and sit-coms thrown in. Customers were dancing, throwing darts, shooting pool, and playing pinball machines. Nick fixed on the TV while Boosty beat Con at darts. As Con drew near, Nick shook his head at the television.

"Another desert country detonating nukes. Excuse me for appearing insensitive, ladies, but folks who still ride camels should not be messing with nuclear fission." Nick poured down his gin and gestured with his emptied glass toward the TV. "And no one speaks American anymore but vaudeville-comic rhythms, inflection rising at the end to key the laugh. Another nail in the cultural coffin. Though like Himmler whenever I hear the word 'Culture' I reach for my revolver."

"To shoot yourself?"

The gin was getting to Con and he wished he hadn't said that, thinking about Hemingway blowing his head off in Idaho. But Nick didn't seem put-off by his query.

"That's the only true philosophic question, Conman, whether or not to pull the trigger. The rest is bullshit."

"It's all bullshit," Bustamante interjected, stirring his gin with a dart then draining it off. "Except for my medication. Barkeeper: another round."

Nick, still focused on the TV, shook his head. "Impotent senators and ballplayers doing ads for prick medicine." He took a swallow of gin as antidote. "Give me the good old days. During the civil war the Madrid whores were giving it away to Anarchists. The women were young, reckless, and anxious to prove their love for humanity."

"Anarchist women?" Con asked, inhaling the scent of juniper from his glass and feeling the cool, burning gin on his tongue.

"An oxymoron, that. Usually Woman's the cure for chaos. The only thing that keeps us civil, for better or worse."

As if to punctuate Nick's point, Nadya jumped up on the bar in her miniskirt, dancing to "Back in the U.S.S.R.," now blasting from the overhead speakers. The dart throwers started tossing dollar bills at her feet and the pool players followed suit. Johannsen began collecting the currency and buying drinks. Nick glanced up Nadya's skirt and looked around the bar.

"This is all well and good for a rainy day, Conman. But if you want to be a working writer you can't do this all the time. A difficult task, though, staying sober in a town with more A.A. chapters than churches. Still, the beauty of pure drunkenness outweighs the infrequent bouts of gastric remorse, always the result of bad company or something like." Nick stared off as if at a distant memory. "Yeah, a real danger on which I could expound. But that's the extent of my lecture today, Conman.

"Meanwhile, I bless and forgive you, my son, for we have all sinned at one time or another and I have taken it upon myself to represent the eternal force and dispense wisdom and absolution without charge or reward. Cheers."

Con raised his glass. Nick was good, almost too good. He could still see no cracks in the Hemingway façade. None. But then, Con's gin-softened mind offered, just maybe it wasn't a façade after all...

Chapter Twenty-one

Next day Con woke to his buzzing cell phone. His land-lord, Berman, calling from Santa Fe about the approaching hurricane, said latest reports indicated a direct Category Two hit on Key West. He asked Con to board up the house and evacuate. The downstairs neighbors were already pack-ing kid and dog into their Volkswagen van, off to visit kin in North Carolina.

Con called Johannsen, who drove him to the lumber-yard, where there was a run on plywood. They got the last few sheets and loaded them into his SUV, along with a circular saw.

The two men were nailing freshly cut woodsy-smelling trapezoids over the front door transom when Eva showed up on the sidewalk.

"What should I do, Cone? They say there will be no electric or water and to go to the shelter on Pine Street."

He looked to Johannsen, who said, "The more the merrier."

Con told her: "Go home and pack some sexy under-wear and come back in an hour. We'll evacuate in style."

They carried the aluminum ladder to the back of the house and Con climbed it to untie canvas awnings that shaded the downstairs deck and upstairs window. From his vantage point atop the ladder the sky looked odd, with low black clouds scudding in against a steel gray backdrop. The wind had picked up a few knots.

Soon he heard a voice calling from out front: "Hey, Conman!"

Nick hulked on the front porch next to Ricardo; Aurora sat on the porch swing. Nick tilted his head toward her and said, "Keep an eye on her for a few days. Ricardo and I are taking the Pilar out of harm's way. I know a key with a shallow-water cove where we can anchor her and ride it out."

Con once again caught the eye of Johannsen, who nodded and said, "Plenty of room at my place. Storm shutters, generator, and lots to drink. We'll enjoy ourselves."

Though Con wasn't so sure. He translated Johannsen's words for Ricardo's and Aurora's benefit, wondering how enjoyable it would be if Eva saw Aurora as a threat. His recent experience with Cat made him sensitive to possible jealousy and competitiveness between the two women. At least he could act as filter and censor, he figured, since Eva spoke no Spanish and Aurora no English.

After a round of mojitos on the front porch, Nick and Ricardo prepared to leave. But before the two men headed off down Elizabeth Street and back to the Pilar, Nick pulled Con aside.

"If anything happens that you don't see me again, Conman, don't forget The Code. Be prepared to work always without applause. You'll be excited about it when the first draft is done. But no one can see it until you have gone over it again and again, until you've communicated the emotion, the sights and the sounds to the reader. And remember," he said, pressing a thick finger into Con's chest, "to submit to the work and the gods you're serving and nothing and no one else. Remember what you're here for."

Then he reached out as if to shake hands but instead pressed into Con's palm a worn white rabbit's foot. With that he was off.

*

Soon Eva showed up wearing wedgies and skimpy cut-offs and pulling a wheeled carry-on bag. Con introduced the two women without explanation.

"Mucho gusto," said Aurora as Eva looked her up and down.

Rain came as the men loaded the bags into the SUV. Con asked: "Is this a good problem or bad problem, Jojo?"

"The hurricane? Depends what you make of it."

"I meant the women."

"Ditto. Just remember you can marry only one."

They followed a line of cars up U.S. 1 and over Cow Key Channel, which separated Key West from neighboring Stock Island. There Johannsen turned right on McDonald Avenue. After a few blocks he pulled the Mercedes into a trailer court and disappeared into a tiny, cream-colored travel trailer wedged between two doublewides. Con sat between Aurora and Eva in the back seat, watching the windshield wipers tilt from side to side.

Eva squeezed his arm and said: "This will be interesting test, to see if we can cohabit."

"Very interesting," he said, feeling Aurora's eyes on him. But he was dreading the situation. Already he sensed a tension between the two women but was thankful they were limited to communicating it with body language and cold glances.

Johannsen came ducking out of the trailer followed by Nadya. He opened the passenger door for her, threw her bag in back, and slid behind the wheel. After making brief introductions in English as he drove, he mouthed something in Russian to Nadya. At which point Eva laid a hand on her shoulder and spoke to her in Russian. Nadya turned and cooed at Eva, and they began to babble away, both obviously excited by the discovery that they had a common tongue.

Then Con heard Aurora clear her throat. "Izveni-tye...," she said and joined in the Russian conversation.

His eyes met Johannsen's in the rearview mirror. Jojo raised his eyebrows, as if to suggest that the Cold War between Eva and Aurora might now heat up.

*

They soon pulled to a stop before Johannsen's Key Haven home. Once inside, Nadya showed the other two women the Gulfside sunset view (now largely obliterated by dark clouds and storm shutters), high-tech appliances and plasma TV.

Con asked Johannsen: "You secure the boat?"

"Not yet."

Eager to absent himself from the domestic enclave, Con volunteered. In the garage downstairs he found a coil of green synthetic line and white plastic bumpers. He moved across the backyard patio in the warm rain, boarded Tailchaser, and began lashing the boat in the middle of the canal, twenty feet from either side, as the rain came harder. He dropped anchors fore and aft then dove in to make sure they were hooked on solid rock. Next he hung bumpers from all the cleats and folded down and secured the bimini.

Johannsen came down the circular metal staircase from the back deck in a rain jacket, a tinned Heineken in either hand. Con swam to the concrete dock and climbed the ladder.

"Hope it holds."

Johannsen shrugged. "It's insured."

Con drank and lifted his chin toward the house. "What

are the girls doing?"

"Aurora's offered to cook dinner, some sort of Cubano-Africano chicken."

"Step one: Sacrifice a rooster."

Johannsen fixed him with a gaze. "Careful with her, Martens. She's beautiful but spooky—those eyes."

"They getting along okay?"

"I just overheard Eva ask Aurora, 'Won't they let you wear makeup in The Workers' Paradise?'"

Con shook his head. "Really wish Nick hadn't dumped Aurora on me. Guess he had his reasons." Con took another pull on his beer. "At least it's good material."

*

Back inside, after donning dry clothes Con found that Eva and Nadya had gone off together to the master bedroom to dress for dinner while Aurora busied herself in the kitchen. With Johannsen following the hurricane's progress on The Weather Channel, Con poured himself a whiskey and sat at the kitchen counter sipping and watching Aurora work.

"Smells delicious."

"A recipe from my black grandmother, a dish for special occasions. But this time con un toque ruso," with a Russian touch, she said with an odd, feline grin. Gazing into her eyes Con felt suddenly chilled.

Soon Nadya and Eva appeared from the bedroom dressed in short leather skirts, spiked heels, skintight tanktops, eyeliner, and lipstick. As Eva made her entrance amid a cloud of perfume, she cast a disparaging look at Aurora's rope sandals. But Aurora moved to the Slavs complimenting their attire in Russian and acting humble and envious.

Aurora prepared the dining table and soon invited everyone to sit. Then as she was serving them plates of chicken and yellow rice the lights flickered and the room went black.

The wind roared outside, encircling the house. Rain pounded the shutters and roof. Then the dark was cut by the glow of a match, which Aurora touched to candles at the center of the table.

Johannsen said, "*Spasiba,* Aurora," and went on in Russian. Then he turned to Con: "Told them I'll wait till after dinner to start up the generator, that they are even more beautiful in candlelight."

"Just keep them smiling." Con attempted one in Eva's direction.

Johannsen rose to pour wine from bottles of Burgundy he grasped in either hand, then lifted his glass. "Na zdrovye!"

After a few bites they all began praising the food in English, Spanish, and Russian. Eva, who sat to Con's left, looked across the table to Aurora on his right, and said something in Russian. Aurora gazed back at her and said, "*Nyet.*"

Con felt Eva's foot stroking his leg as she went on while the others listened. When she finished, Aurora laid down her fork, dabbed her lips with her napkin, and began a Russian monologue that lasted two minutes, speaking evenly and, seemingly, dispassionately. Eva listened with a bemused look and, when Aurora fell silent, shrugged and went back to her chicken. Con looked to Johannsen.

"A discussion of moral philosophy," he explained. "Eva asked if all Cuban women sell themselves to Europeans as they once did to Americans. Which led to a broader discussion on what constitutes a whore. Aurora suggested that some women can sleep with only one man and be a whore while others can have relations with many and remain pure. Then she added that…"

"I get the gist."

The Russian conversation between Eva and Aurora

continued sporadically throughout dinner with, Con detected, a certain sharpness. But he remained gratefully ignorant of its substance, focusing on his meal and his wine. But thanks to the tension at the table the food began to grow bitter on his tongue and the wine acidic.

Outside the wind intensified. As they sipped after-dinner snifters of Cognac a loud thud resounded back of the elevated house. Con looked across to Johannsen.

"I better go check the boat."

*

Con grabbed a rain jacket, flashlight, and coil of line, and pushed his way out the back door. He moved down the circular staircase grasping the wet metal rail. Warm rain stung his face. The wind blew at sixty knots, circling around from the northeast. He turned away to shield his eyes from the wind and water. An ominous darkness loomed: no streetlights; homes shuttered, abandoned, powerless.

The wind whooshed the palms and whistled past the shutters, creating a wavering din like jet engines revving. Licking rain from his lips he shot a beam of light across the back lawn to the pier and moved to the canal, leaning against the wind. A plastic trashcan lid rolled across his path like a ghostly unicycle, chased by palm fronds and beer cans. The water in the canal had risen a foot, but Tailchaser bobbed benignly on the dark brine where he'd lashed her. He checked the cleats and all seemed to be holding, all the lines secure.

Then as he turned back to the house he heard a crack like gunfire, sensed a sharp vibration shoot up his legs from the concrete, and jumped back. He cast light to the ground. There on the pier Con spied a coconut propelled from the tall palm next to the house. Not unlike Cat's bullet, it had likely missed his brain by inches. An unfilled potential that brought a cold laugh to his throat, stifled by the wind and rain. How ignominious to have been killed by a projectile coconut, he thought, after dodging Cat's gunfire, the Cuban Navy, and bull sharks. He reached up to touch the cowrie-shell talisman around his neck. Maybe Aurora's African magic actually worked. Maybe his gods and goddesses had returned. They had gotten him this far. Maybe they would get him further. Maybe his luck had changed. He reached into his pocket and touched the rabbit's foot Nick had given him.

The flying coconut also put his current situation into proper perspective. Hard to take seriously the ire of jealous women—at least those unarmed—when life remained as always so potentially perilous.

*

He marched back upstairs, the metal steps ringing beneath his feet, pulled open the door with both hands, and slid into the darkened room. Now all was quiet. Johannsen and Nadya had apparently gone off to bed. Aurora too had seemingly gone to her room. Eva, he saw, lay curled on the couch. When he sat beside her she did not open her eyes.

"I am not well," she said, holding her stomach.

From the refrigerator he fetched her bottled water and from the bedroom a blanket, with which he covered her. He went to bed thinking that this episode, like Hurricane Hector, would soon pass and was asleep moments after his head found the pillow.

But it was intermittent sleep as the wind played various tunes on the storm shutters—the pitch always rising—and the rain came and went in waves. Blown debris banged against the metal shutters. He heard water rushing through the streets and beneath the elevated home, which trembled in the storm's onslaught, as if it might be ripped from its foundation and washed to sea. When the winds suddenly quieted, Con figured that the benign eye of the storm now passed over them. He still heard the water sluicing outside, but the wind had stilled and the rain had ceased.

Then he sensed a noise not outside but in the room. And another. He opened his eyes to find Aurora standing at the foot of the bed beside a lone, flickering candle she had placed on the floor, naked except for cowrie-shell necklace and ankle bracelet. In her hands she held a length of the green nylon marine line. She came to him and with the line tied his hands together, tethering them to the brass bedstead. Then she lay her palm on his cowrie necklace.

"Dieziséis," she said, "dieziséis. Sixteen shells. And sixteen times we will make love. Then tomorrow let your orishas guide you and your sins be none. And we both shall be pure."

As he lay transfixed staring at her, she began to chant in a new voice—not the sweet warbling of song but a throaty growl. He couldn't make heads or tails of her words; they sounded Spanish but made no sense. Once, he thought she was beseeching the sea, for he heard the phrase "*de la mare*" repeated. But then he realized it was "Olodumare," the Santería God, whom she summoned. And Yemayá, Virgen de Regla, Goddess of the Sea. Then she began to dance.

Her hips swung in slow arcs, the triangle of spare pubic hair, raven and tightly curled, moving toward him and then away. Her dark nipples pointed and firm, lips parted, tongue dancing from her mouth then retreating.

She turned to show him the taut fullness of her hips, the svelte smoothness of her pinched waist, the brown beauty of her flesh. Outside, the hurricane's howl suddenly returned, seemingly heightened.

Her scent came to him—coconut, sweat, and sex. She knelt on the foot of the bed, still writhing. When she bent back, her long, curling black hair fell to the bed. He sensed himself growing erect and her eyes fell there.

Still chanting she reached up to lay her palm on his naked stomach. Con felt a convulsion of lust cut across him, a sexual seasickness deep inside. His ears rang. His skin tingled. His soul seemed to slip into another place. It all seemed so surreal that he wasn't sure whether he was dreaming or awake.

Arms held out to her sides as if for balance, she bent forward slowly, ever so slowly, still dancing to some inner rhythm, to touch her lips to him, then her tongue.

He watched transfixed. Nothing escaped him: no detail, no scent, no sound, no sensation. She moved forward on her knees, still writhing to the silent song inside her, hands still circling at her sides as if swimming through the candlelit night, straddling him, moving closer and closer. Then for an instant she hovered over him, dead still, staring down into his eyes, and now lowered herself onto him. As she enveloped him, a rush of animal pleasure stopped his breath.

She began now to move anew, with a smooth, sinuous motion, her dark flesh like the night sea. Chanting, she threw back her head, eyes rolling back so he could see only their whites, as if she peered deep inside herself. Her body moved like a black tide in which he longed to drown. He smelled her, the scent of woman and warm sex, and felt as if he was about to come, but did not. He moved his hips to meet her thrusts. Her body writhed like waves lapping at the shore, back and forth, back and forth. Thus they remained locked, her sliding up and down on him, Con at the moment of completion but not completing, minute upon minute, hour after hour. Fifteen times he sensed he was about to finish, and she marked each one:

"*Uno...Dos...Tres. ... Trece...Catorce...Quince.*"

He felt time altering, compressing and stretching, it too undulating, pulling him away from himself to an island that only he and Aurora inhabited. And then at the darkened dawn, as the first gray sliver of daylight sliced through the shuttered window on the east, he exploded into her, and she melted into his arms as if liquid.

Chapter Twenty-two

Hurricane Hector ultimately disappeared, leaving nothing of himself, only residual signs of his power. The same with Aurora.

Con slept most of the following day and when he awoke in late afternoon learned that she was gone. Johannsen said she'd apparently slipped out early, for when he and Nadya rose at nine, only Eva remained, asleep on the couch, still recovering from whatever potion or curse Aurora had devised for her.

Con couldn't say for sure what had happened that night, so he told no one. Perhaps he'd been placed in a trance. Or maybe he'd dreamed the whole thing. No, it was too real, too pleasurable, too compelling. Whichever, Aurora had vanished as if she'd left the island on the wind. But he was left with a new sense of purpose, as if she had bestowed upon him an urgency and energy for his book.

However, in the aftermath of Hurricane Hector a depression hung over the island—not a tropical depression but an over-cloud of ennui. The first week was the worst: no power or potable running water, dusk-to-dawn curfews, troops patrolling the island with machine guns, and ten-foot-high piles of downed debris and garbage rotting in the streets. Like living in a Third World dictatorship, Con saw. Back at his home on Elizabeth Street, he wrote in longhand, pen on paper, and spent nights sitting alone without ice for cocktails or cold beer, eating canned tuna, sipping warm whiskey, and reading by candlelight.

He revisited *A Moveable Feast* and saw the young Hemingway writing longhand in Parisian cafes. He saw his own book mounting slowly, for it was construction, not interior decoration, laying one brick at a time. It reminded him of his own early days as a writer, when he was young and full of hope and worked scrawling his scenes in notebooks, when he felt as if he were on a sanctified mission. That sense of purpose now returned in full.

Nick too had vanished, at least materially. However, Nick—or perhaps it was Hemingway himself—came to Con at night. Once, after he had trouble falling asleep for thinking about his book, Nick appeared in his dreams saying, "Don't worry about it, Conman, you'll just bitch yourself. As soon as you start to think about it, stop it. Think about something else. You have to learn that. That way your subconscious will be working on it."

So Con stopped thinking about his work in the evening and worked only mornings, when he was fresh, always stopping when he still had something left in him without completing a scene, so he could pick up the next day and hit the ground running.

He checked the Pilar's slip at Key West Harbor daily and inquired at the Immigration office. But Aurora, Nick, and Ricardo had all departed from his life as suddenly as they had entered it, and he was starting to wonder if they had all been ghosts or hallucinations. With them went any hope of cutting himself in on sunken Spanish treasure, as Nick had seemingly promised, improbable as that now seemed. But he didn't really care now that he was working. Something would turn up.

*

As it turned out, Con's trip to Immigration did pay an unexpected if somewhat melancholy dividend.

As he idled about the office studying wanted posters while waiting his turn, he sensed eyes on him and glanced to his right. There stood a woman in pinstriped suit, carrying a briefcase and staring at him from ten feet. She said:

"Aren't you the writer who's helping Catherine with her novel?"

He stepped toward her. "Do I know you?"

"I was with her the night you met. Back now on another pro bono case."

"I haven't seen Cat for a while," he said. "Guess Hector kept her away."

"You mean Nestor."

"Hurricane Nestor?"

She laughed. "Sorry. I thought you meant her husband. They're off visiting his folks in Moscow. Should be back next week."

Con looked away, gazing off at the photos of men wanted for smuggling, terrorism, and international flight, but seeing instead a picture clarifying in his mind. "That explains everything...By the way, has Nestor gotten his Green Card yet?"

"Another six months."

Con nodded repeatedly. That's why she never invited him to Miami and was so reticent about her private life. And why she was so insanely jealous and possessive—since she herself was possessed, entrapped in a seemingly altruistic and perhaps non-conjugal dead-end marriage to the Russian. Which would also explain her sexual voraciousness.

"Give her my regards," he said, "and tell her I want to hear all about their trip."

This was good news, he told himself. Cat's being married let him off the hook for two-timing and dumping her. He should have felt vindicated. But instead the news left him hollow and blue. Maybe he'd been in love with her after all. He just never knew it. And he realized she was the other one he was writing for.

Chapter Twenty-three

Despite post-hurricane stress and penury, Con generally felt euphoric, for he was working again, writing the book he'd told Aurora about when pressed: The story of the decadent Americano encountering a sexy santera in Havana who changes his life. As they said, write about what you know. And maybe it was a true story not fiction, he thought. Maybe the witch did put a beneficent, life-altering spell on him before she vanished. He felt the magic and mystery of creation returning to him.

The raw material at his disposal—all he had experienced and read and heard tell—served but as base elements to an alchemy that transformed them, altered by secret rituals that seeped from his subconscious as from the gods. In his material he saw depths he had not before plumbed, crystalline meaning that had once been obscure, beauty he had not previously appreciated. He saw the parallel struggles of the fictional santera in his novel and the American protagonist intersect beyond time; he viewed their individual disintegration, renewal and reunion as both unpredictable yet, retrospectively, inevitable.

Con saw, too, Nick's absence as purposeful. A time comes for a writer—after all the study, reading, musing, agonizing, suffering, dreaming, plotting, planning and advice, to sit down and write and let the best parts of you pour onto the page. Though Nick was absent, Con sensed his presence, felt him looking over his shoulder and took his counsel at night in his dreams—at least at first. Then Nick became ubiquitous.

One morning Con wrote a paragraph of which he was particularly proud for its evocative and poetic prose, its literary allusions to Odysseus and other sailors, its intellectual rigor and depth. But as he sat basking in the glow of his words and looked up from his computer screen, he saw Nick leaning against the door jamb of the verandah, puffing on his pipe and slowly shaking his head. Con looked again at the paragraph, literally blushed, and quickly deleted it.

He knew it was just his imagination summoning up images of Nick. But he also saw that writing for Nick—as well as for himself and for Cat—helped strengthen his novel.

One night, unable to push thoughts of his story from his mind before sleep, he thought to clear his head by stating aloud: "The power of the santera is daunting, Nick. She's scary and keeps slipping away from me. One character I can't pin down."

That night he dreamt of Nick at the helm of the Pilar, staring out across the sunlit Gulf Stream as the two of them trolled for marlin. "All women are priestesses, Conman, or goddesses and thus ultimately unknowable," the dream-Nick said. "The only way to pin them down is to prick them. And even then they disappear on you. Write down what you saw when she made you feel that way, what you smelled, the way she moved and the depths of her eyes, the concrete things that produced the emotion of fear and then your readers will feel that fear as well. Don't talk about the feeling, don't beg it. Just observe and report."

The next morning when he woke he did as Nick had instructed. From then on Con began directly asking advice of Nick in absentia, talking to him, and Nick responded, one way or another.

*

Running low on cash, Con turned to his writing students. Still no word from Sandra after her Cuba trip. Rebecca Hemingway didn't answer her phone. He'd left a message for Marta at the newspaper days earlier but had gotten no reply. But finally one morning she called saying she needed to see him.

He unlocked his mountain bike from the chain-link fence downstairs and pedaled east on Fleming Street, moving up island toward Garrison Bight, counting on another forty bucks from her for the coaching session. A calm, sunlit day in Paradise, as the Chamber of Commerce called it. Albeit a decidedly American as opposed to biblical paradise, with drugs, loud music, strip joints, and noisy motor scooters. The last in evidence as a group of college kids zipped past him sounding horns.

At the Bight he coasted down the dock to Marta's houseboat, locked his Trek to a potted palm on the front deck, and called through the screen door. She appeared, padding barefoot across the kitchen linoleum in baggy shorts and tee shirt, as if to conceal her advancing shapelessness. As he stepped inside she put a hand on his shoulder, covering the tattoo of a scorpion he got one drunken night in Puerto Escondido, and stood on tiptoe to press her cheek to his. Though not yet noon he could smell the booze on her. Her eyes were red though not just from drinking.

"You been crying?"

"The bastards."

"Which?"

"Have a drink with me."

She led him into the bedroom, where her manuscript sat in short stacks on the sheets. On the dresser he spied a vodka bottle and a plate of halved-oranges. She plopped cross-legged on the bed and began rifling through one of the stacks.

"You've got to help me organize this thing, Con. I've got to get an advance."

He studied her to see if she was serious, as if advances on first books were as common as carpenter ants in Key West. Her concept wasn't bad: a true crime tome about a woman tourist who went home with the wrong guy, who sodomized her with a lead pipe and threw her bloodless body in a dumpster. A story Marta had originally covered for *The Key West Citizen*. But thanks to her drinking she had trouble finishing eight-hundred-word stories for the newspaper much less an eighty-thousand-word book.

"Why the hurry?"

"Miss one fucking deadline..."

One *more* fucking deadline, he tacitly corrected her. "They can you?" He bit his tongue so as not to add "finally."

"I get unemployment for six months but that's it. If I can't get an advance I'll have to find a job somewhere else. I'll lose my home, my friends,...¡Ay de mí!"

He sat on the navy blue sheets and looked across to her. Her black hair lay shining on her shoulders. Her hands shook almost imperceptibly. She wasn't a bad writer when sober and a good pal with or without the vodka. A plain-looking yet bright woman, the daughter of working-class Cuban émigrés. But for some reason she had trouble believing in herself—like a lot of working-class kids, he knew from personal experience. Studying her manuscript she pressed fingers to her lips as she often did—a nervous habit that seemed to express self-doubt about what issued from those lips, an innate insecurity that also manifested itself in vodka, as if to numb those lips and that self-doubt.

A so-called laughing gull landed on the Astroturf deck just beyond the sliding screen door and emitted a piercing ha ha haah. Beyond the gull gray pelicans paddled in blue-green water at the dock's end. A fishing boat chugged past, heading out the channel to the Gulf of Mexico. The scent of the oranges came to him.

"Advances ain't that easy, Marta. But we can try. Hone the first few chapters and work on a proposal to send round to agents. You never know."

And you never did know. She had talent. And she had a good start. But she also had a hard time believing she could actually do it. Afraid of relinquishing who she was, even if it was a failure. The same struggle he had gone through.

"Just keep driving on the book, Marta, living in it. Focus and discipline. It'll come," he said, words that were as much a prayer for his own project as coaching.

She buried her head in his chest and began sobbing, her tears feeling cool as they dropped to his forearm.

"But I can't pay you, Con. I know I need help but can't afford it."

He looked down at the manuscript scattered across the sheets, realizing what a long shot it was for her. But it seemingly was the only shot she had.

"It's okay. I don't need your money. We'll work on it together…But with conditions."

She looked up at him, and Con took a deep breath.

"You know, Marta, even Hemingway himself admitted that his work suffered when he lost his work ethic, when he started drinking too much…"

Chapter Twenty-four

Hurricane season brought more threats, but after Hector the island got off easy. A couple tropical storms dumped down torrential rain in September. A scare in October with a Category Four storm, Patricia, that veered off into the Gulf just as Con was getting ready to board up again. But now, at the end of October, hurricane season had pretty much passed. The only thing left for Con to dodge was the weeklong Fantasy Fest, when a hundred thousand drunken sybarites invaded the island. He wanted to evacuate to the relative sanity of the Midwest to see some fall color, but the money Nick had given him hadn't gone far. Again Con was tapped out and trapped, unable to afford even a plane ticket. But the work went well on his novel, and that was all that really mattered, he told himself.

However, his overarching good mood was dampened one day by a letter in his mailbox: a job offer from a University of Texas campus on the Mexican border, beginning in January, teaching fiction-writing to bilingual students.

He'd forgotten that he'd even applied for it last spring, when thoroughly desperate. Though he now remembered getting a letter from them after a telephone interview, stating they'd filled the position. But whomever they originally picked apparently had had enough after one semester and was already bailing out.

The job offer put him in a funk because he knew he should take it: sixty thousand dollars for nine months work. But there was no snorkeling in the Chihuahuan Desert, no beaches with palm trees, no babes in bikinis. And, most important, no leisure what with grading papers, meeting with eager students you couldn't say "No" to, and attending soporific committee meetings called to boost some colleague's ego. He'd been there, and recalled Nabokov's words to Edmund Wilson before he struck it rich with *Lolita*: "I am sick of teaching, I am sick of teaching, I am sick of teaching."

And of course this would surface at the moment Con had actually started writing again. As always, Fate fucking with him, though he knew he wasn't special in that regard.

To score some cash he again tried calling Rebecca Hemingway, though with some trepidation. From day to day she could display any one of several personas, from charming and playful cynic to depressed, whining pessimist. And if you got her on the wrong day it could be hell. But he heard a recording: "That number is no longer in service…"

Her studio sat in the rear of a rehabbed Conch house only a few blocks away, so he strolled over as the sun set and climbed the back stairs. The house was owned by a rich old New York art dealer for whom Rebecca acted as personal secretary and who gave her the apartment in exchange. Each time Con saw her for a lesson she seemed to have a new job doing this or that kind of office work around town but always paid him promptly in cash. When he knocked on the screen door he heard her voice through it:

"I told you to stay away."

He thought of retreating but then called through the screen: "It's me, Con."

He heard rustling but no further response. After a minute she came to the door in a black silk robe, smoking a cigarette, and looked him up and down.

"Thought it was someone else."

She unhooked the screen door and retreated back into the dim room. He followed. Clothes, books, and CDs lay scattered on the carpet, the bed unmade.

She wasn't in much better shape than the room. Hair uncombed, as if she'd just risen from bed, her complexion pallid. Atop the bookcase by the kitchenette sat a framed photo of a smiling, bespectacled teenager, round-faced and innocent: Rebecca before. Rebecca after had sunken cheeks, dark circles under her eyes as if she'd not slept, and no trace of a smile. She stood surveying the items strewn about the room as if trying to decide what to do with it all. Finally she said:

"You want my laptop? It's new."

"Don't you need it for your book?"

"I'm not writing a book. I'm dying." Her eyes met his gaze. "Ovarian cancer. Here, take the computer."

She looked away as Con studied her. "When did all this happen?"

"What difference does it make?"

"Can't they do something?"

"No health insurance. Don't worry. I won't die of cancer."

He sat on the edge of the striped loveseat, atop week-old newspapers, feeling a burning in his throat. "Meaning you plan to kill yourself?"

She moved to the kitchen and poured a cup from the coffeemaker. "You want coffee?"

Con shook his head. "You been sleeping?"

She turned to him, hot coffee sloshing onto her fingers, but she seemed to take no notice. "What's sleep?"

"And food?"

She looked down to her bare feet, tears welling in her eyes. She turned to hide them.

Con said: "Let me take you to dinner."

"I can't go anywhere. Not like this."

*

They agreed to meet in a half hour at a place near the south end of Simonton Street, where they served good fish and Cuban food. He decided to walk over, strolling first to South Beach to kill a few minutes. There he meandered out onto the long concrete pier, dark water lapping at either side. He gazed west, where the sun had set but the sky still shone aquamarine along the horizon. Such a beautiful world, he thought, and such a short time to embrace it. Then a long time dead. Why anyone would want to rush it...

He was already dreading what figured to be a somber dinner, his hasty invitation born out of a sudden sympathy for her. But if she was in fact dying or fixing to, maybe this would be the last time he'd see her alive. Besides, it could be good material, he told himself, the universal excuse that justified most anything for writers.

They sat at a Formica-topped table. He thought to ask her: "You know a guy named Nick Adams? Thought he might be a relative. Lives on a fishing boat in the harbor and claims to be Hemingway reincarnate."

"I know twenty like him, thinking they're the new Hemingway or Robert Frost."

The waitress ambled over with a smile and asked Rebecca, "Can I get you a drink, Honey?"

"Don't call me 'Honey,'" Rebecca snapped. "I'm not a child."

The waitress reddened, turned, and strode away. Rebecca, now sheepish, offered: "Guess I shouldn't have said that, huh?"

"Unless you intended to be a bona fide bitch. She's just trying to make a living. Jesus Christ, Rebecca. Life's tough enough."

"Tell me about it."

He looked across at her. Hard to feel for her but he did anyway. "Don't you have family that can help?"

"That's a laugh."

Family: That's what fucked her up in the first place, she contended in her book, which described how Ernest Hemingway's looming legend had poisoned her life. Thanks to the mystique of the Hemingway name and her father's identifying with his distant celebrity kin, he took off to live large but ended up drinking himself to death in Mexico. Her mother, deprived of the ease and luxury she thought she'd married into and wallowing in self-pity, turned bitter. To compensate for her disappointment she sent four-year-old Rebecca into department stores to steal jewelry and perfume for her.

"You talk to your mother?"

"Three years ago. No idea where she is and don't care."

That, at least, was a healthy attitude, he thought, given how Mom had used her.

Finally after ten minutes a new waitress arrived and took their order in a businesslike way. In another minute she returned with two glasses of white wine. When she left, Con said:

"Why not see a social worker and get some help. The hospital won't turn you away. Maybe you could go to Cuba for cheapie surgery."

She took a swallow of wine. "Those are fine ideas for someone with the will to live."

He sipped his wine, which lay bitter on his tongue. "You know that comes and goes. Right now you're depressed and not making good decisions. Maybe you should postpone doing anything rash on the chance you'll snap out of it. Never know what's around the corner. Maybe a miracle." He reached into his pocket to rub his rabbit's foot, trying to summon one for himself as well.

She looked at him with heavy eyelids and swallowed. "Sure." Then she went back to her wine.

Soon their food was delivered without comment. He ate, wondering how she planned to do it. Pills most likely. Or the long swim. Sometimes people just disappeared from Key West, and you never knew if they won the lottery and moved to France or just got tired of it all and decided to backstroke to Bimini. But the hints were all there in her book, *Smoking the Bible*—the title taken, at his suggestion, from her 90-day stint in the Los Angeles County jail for passing bad checks. There, for lack of cigarettes, she smoked dried orange peels rolled in pages torn from a Gideon Bible.

"You talk to anybody about all this?"

"You mean my shrink? Lot of help she's been. No one cares."

He stabbed his fried mahi with his fork. "Well, I'm a victim too. Of class warfare and clueless parents. Of inept high-school counseling and raging hormones. Where's my free pass?"

She toyed with her food. "Yeah, life sucks."

Con lay down his fork. "Particularly if you're a brat and a coward. If you haven't the mettle to stand and fight the bastards."

"What if you're one of the bastards?"

Con shook his head. "I don't see it, Rebecca. Yeah, you drew the short straw in some ways and as a result you've done some wicked things. But we all have. You aren't as bad as you think you are."

Which led him down another street: And you, Constantine Martens, are likely not as good as you think, your self-love perhaps just as misguided as her self-loathing, albeit less damaging. Rebecca was a lost soul. And, as with most folks who were screwed up, it was just too bad. Not much you could do about it. Up to them. Though she was right about one thing: No one would care once she was gone. She tainted most everything she touched, ultimately alienated everyone she met, and was letting herself go physically and mentally. Still, he couldn't bring himself to brush her off as he knew he should.

"Rebecca…Call me anytime. If there's anything I can do. Even if you just need to talk."

She chewed her lip and nodded.

When the bill came she grabbed it, paid, and left a big tip. Outside on the sidewalk Con wished her, "Bon voyage."

She looked at him as if checking to see if he was being ironic, got on her motor scooter without a word, and buzzed off down the dark avenue.

*

He walked back up Elizabeth Street in the warm night, thinking that he shouldn't have tried to talk her out of suicide. Not only would it put her out of her misery but, more important, it would save the planet another petulant shit who went around spoiling it for others.

Suddenly on the night air he heard voices singing:

> …Children go where I send thee.
> How shall I send thee?

Ahead he saw light falling onto the dim street from the Church of God of Prophecy and moved toward it. Inside under bright light worshipers swayed as they sang, the piano vibrating the slat floor.

> I'm gonna send you four by four,
> Four for the four who stood at the door,
> Three for the Hebrew children,

Two for Paul and Silas,
And one for the little bitty baby
Who was born, born, born in Bethlehem.

Chapter Twenty-five

Con witnessed something ugly that he wished he hadn't seen. Next morning, biking around the island, he stopped at Kmart to buy some tennis balls. In the sporting goods department at the back of the store he heard a shrill voice going on about shoddy work, sloth, and absenteeism. He moved down the aisle and, just outside the storeroom doors, spied a woman dressing down Paolo. Con stepped back.

He hadn't known that Paolo had returned from Cuba. But there he was, staring at the floor, shifting his weight from foot to foot, gripping the handle of his wide dust mop as if to strangle it. The tongue lashing finally ended, and the woman strode off. Paolo turned and disappeared into the storeroom pulling his dust mop behind him, head lowered as if wishing he could vanish. The woman came striding down the aisle where Con stood. He stepped toward her.

"You the store manager?"

She stopped and eyed him with suspicion. "Assistant manager."

Con nodded. "I think you've reached your level of incompetence. Good luck, and may God bless you."

She gazed at him slack-jawed. He pivoted and made for the checkout without waiting for a reply.

No, he wished he hadn't seen that. But it told him that since Paolo was back from his trip, Sandra was too. He decided to give her a call to see if he could pry another hundred-dollar lesson out of her.

*

That afternoon he was driving up U.S. 1 to Sugarloaf Key and Sandra's place in Johannsen's Porsche, which he was happy to loan Con just to give it some exercise.

When he'd called Sandra, she mentioned nothing about a lesson re her kiss-and-tell memoir but invited him up for a drink, saying she had good news. But even if she had no cash for him, life was good. He had the top down on the Porsche, the sun shone, and on either side of the highway lay the pale aquamarine waters that looked so phony in Keys travel ads. But he was still thinking about poor Paolo and remembered their conversation that led, ultimately, to Eva leaving her thong under his bed, Cat pulling the gun on him and his meeting Nick.

One night at the Bayview Park tennis courts he had run into Paolo, who had a good if unorthodox game and loved America. Back in the Czech Republic, where he'd made two hundred bucks a month as a baker, tennis courts cost ten dollars an hour. Here he made two thousand dollars a month and tennis courts were free. Thus his burgeoning Americanism.

After three sets under the lights, Paolo—strikingly handsome and dark-haired—pulled two bottles of Staropramen beer from his canvas cooler as they sat on the bleachers.

"My van…" He lifted his beer bottle toward a twenty-year-old Ford Econoline parked on U.S. 1 adjacent to the pedestrian crossing. "…It needs thousand-dollar transmission work to make reverse. I earn twelve dollars an hour sweeping Kmart. So I am clever how to park."

A twin-engine turboprop roared past a couple hundred feet overhead, dropping toward the Key West airport. When it was quiet except for the traffic streaming by, Paolo went on:

"And now Mirella is gone."

"Your girlfriend from Czecho?"

"Together we come to Key West two years ago. Now she leaves me for American."

"That's tough, Paolo."

"And last night I spend in jail."

Paolo explained that he was so distraught over his straying lover that he called her father back in the Czech Republic to tell him of his faithless progeny, a stripper at one of the Duval Street clubs. When Mirella showed up to collect her clothes, Paolo boasted how he had ratted her out to her father, and she slapped his face for it. So Paolo put her over his knee and spanked her, as her father had advised. However, the spanking infuriated instead of soothing Mirella, who pitched a beer bottle at Paolo's head, which he ducked.

"Then," Paolo said, "she takes ka-feen…" He made stabbing motions.

"A knife?"

"Yes, ka-nife from kitchen and comes at me." He stabbed the air some more.

He managed to disarm her and throw her outside, where she found a rock to toss through the window. Then she called 911 on her cell phone. The cops showed and arrested Paolo for assault, thus Mirella was able to collect her clothes. Next morning Johannsen posted a fifteen-hundred-dollar bond to spring him.

They opened two more Staros and drank in silence.

After a minute Con said:

"Forget Mirella. What you need is a rich American girl-friend with a powerboat to teach you English and take you fishing."

"You know this woman?"

"Absolutely," he said, thinking of Sandra and her forty-foot Bayliner. "American chicks dig foreign accents. She might even pay for your transmission work."

Paolo knocked his beer bottle against Con's. "And for you I find Czech girlfriend. I know all the strippers."

*

A half hour up the Keys, Con hung a left on an asphalt road that twisted for a mile till it dead-ended. Then right on a gravel drive winding through silver palms and giving out on a turnaround before a three-story house surround-ed by lanky queen palms. Sandra's blue BMW convertible sat in the garage.

As he rose from the Porsche, Con sensed humid air smelling of the sea. He trotted up the stairs to the deck that circled the house, knocked, and called through the screen door. He walked around to the east side of the house and looked out over the mangroves and down the boardwalk to the green sea and boat dock. There he spied Sandra in a hammock under the canvas canopy, her power-boat moored beyond.

He moved over the boardwalk, which perched above rocky tidal flats dotted with scrub, and crossed the hun-dred yards to the dock. When she heard his footfall she lifted her head.

"Constantine."

"Hello, Sandra," he said—pronouncing it Sawn-drah, as she did—and saw that she was naked in the hammock, her bottle-blonde hair pinned up on her head. She was a tan, slender woman of forty- or fifty- or sixty-something who occasionally flew to Buenos Aires for renovations.

Her breasts looked young and pert, her light-brown pubic hair nicely coiffed. But her face looked tight, as if she might have trouble smiling.

She told him to help himself to a beer from the cooler beside her. He fished a Heineken from the ice, pulled up a canvas deck chair, and sat facing her, thinking again of Paolo and the likely contrast between his days in Cuba with Sandra and his morning with the bitch at Kmart.

"Last time we talked you two were headed to Havana."

"Bimini. He'd had his fill of the Workers' Paradise back in Budapest or wherever. Cuba didn't sound like much of a vacation. Besides, that was weeks ago." She reached across to lay a cool hand on his arm—a coolness that seemed to mark her. She ran a few degrees below normal in most ways. "Listen, Con. There's wonderful news: I've gotten a contract on my book."

The green bottle halfway to his lips, he said, "With a publisher?"

"Random House. Can't believe how quickly it happened."

"Thought you weren't going to send it around till it was finished."

"At the marina in Bimini I met an agent from William Morris. He looked at my manuscript and asked to take it with him. Then just last night I finally got a call from him. I'm flying up to New York next week to meet my editor and sign papers."

Con nodded, pursing his lips and thinking how she must have fucked the agent's socks off—something most writers would do to get published. Still, he knew about the vagaries of publishing, how luck played a part, and how he himself had benefited by it, at least in the short run. So, no hundred-dollar lesson today. However, he told himself not to be small about it but to welcome her good fortune, to which he had made a substantive contribution with his coaching.

"That's great news, Sandra."

"Isn't it? I feel like celebrating, Con. Let's go up to the house for Champagne."

She wrapped an orange sarong around her waist and strode, barefoot and topless under a wide straw hat, up the boardwalk. He followed, watching her hips sway under the sarong and thinking of the presidents, anchormen, rock stars, ballplayers and even Czech janitors who had enjoyed her.

"Sandra, I was thinking: Maybe you can use Paolo as a working-class interlude in your book."

She glanced over her shoulder as she strolled. "Who?"

Chapter Twenty-six

Still no actual sign of Nick or Aurora. Eva, however, persisted in her campaign to marry him, supported by Johannsen's paramour Nadya, now Eva's best friend. The two women, Con saw, had so much in common: the Russian language, a sexworker Weltanschauung, and Green-Card ambitions.

That evening he was sitting on the verandah re-reading Hemingway's early, Nick Adams stories when he heard a pounding on the hooked screen door downstairs. Then a chorus calling his name. He descended to find Johannsen, Nadya, and Eva decked out for Fantasy Fest and drinking cocktails from plastic cups.

Johannsen, bare-chested, wore sandals and a sarong. Nadya and Eva likewise were topless, though with breasts painted: Nadya's as two red Soviet flags to match her red tanga, Eva's as a leopard-skin bra to match her swimsuit bottom. Both wore spangled eye-masks and high heels. All three were happily tipsy. Eva lifted her cup to Con's lips and bade him drink.

"Come, Cone. The parade is starting."

Nadya meanwhile was reaching under Johannsen's sarong and giggling. Johannsen, in response, danced a hula. Con savored the tequila and lime Eva offered.

"Why not?" he replied to Eva's invitation. "How often will this happen in the Chihuahuan Desert?" But no one was paying attention.

*

At a liquor store on Fleming Street Johannsen bought a pint of tequila, and they refilled their cups on the sidewalk. On Duval Street thick crowds lined both sides of the parade route: beer-bellied men in jock straps and topless women, both thick and thin, with breasts painted to resemble cats' eyes, Big Macs, bloodhound ears, and the Milky Way. Floats addressing that year's theme, "Underwater Fantasies," rolled by peopled by men in drag or sporting fake phalluses and near-naked, body-painted women tossing beads and candy to onlookers. Music blared from the floats and the spectators cheered. The aromas of perfume, liquor, beer, and sweat hovered in the warm night air.

Johannsen called to Con over the din: "This is great!"

"I don't get it."

"You would if you worked nine-to-five. It's Saturnalia for these folks. Their annual brush with the wild twin left behind at birth."

The four of them moved up the block toward the Atlantic Ocean. They passed a man dressed as a physician, with white lab coat and stethoscope, holding a placard that read: "Free Breast Examinations." Nadya stopped to take him up on it, and others in the crowd turned their video cams on the "doctor" as he groped her Soviet flags. This put Eva in a playful mood as well, and she moved Con's hand to her breast as they strolled on through the pressing crowd.

On one passing float they spied a man, perhaps eighty, carrying a video cam and sporting a tee shirt that read, "Show Me Your Tits!"

Con turned to Johannsen. "I need that shirt for departmental meetings."

Johannsen, eyeing a woman next to him lifting her tank-top to accommodate the old man with the video cam, asked, "What departmental meetings?"

"Got a midterm job-offer teaching creative writing."

"Where?"

"University of Texas-Butthole-Border-Town Campus."

"You're not considering it?"

"That or sleep under the mangroves."

"You wouldn't last a semester."

"I've no choice."

"Nothing coming in?"

"Nada."

"I won't allow it. Move in with me until you can find a job. Go on welfare. Just don't go to Texas. Without water you'll wither and die."

Eva slipped her arm around Con's waist as they walked and licked sweat from his biceps before swilling more tequila.

"I have to do something."

"What about Eva's offer?"

Con swallowed down more liquor as Eva put the bottle to his lips.

"Still on the table."

A woman walked by in an open hospital gown with white Band-Aids painted on either nipple of perfectly round, grapefruit-sized breasts, along with the inked announcement, "Brand New!"

"That would buy you time to finish your novel."

"Seems so mercenary."

Johannsen looked at him. "Your point being?"

They pushed on through the perspiring, booze-soaked crowd. Having finished off the tequila, Johannsen and Nadya drifted off to find more. Eva writhed against Con, pressing her lips to his.

The feel of her warm body and her scent heated his blood. They moved arm-in-arm away from the crowds down a dark side street and along a high brick wall that guarded a two-storey stone mansion with wrought-iron balconies: the Hemingway House. A wedding gift from Pauline's uncle when they married in '28, Con knew, complete with saltwater pool and servants. There Hem had produced some of his most renowned work: *Death in the Afternoon, For Whom the Bell Tolls*, "The Snows of Kilimanjaro," and other stories. While he himself, Con saw, had produced nothing in his hand-to-mouth Key West sojourn.

In the blackness Eva leaned against the brick wall, tugged at his zipper, and reached into his shorts. Placing a high heel on an overturned blue plastic recycling bin, she lifted aside her fake-leopard thong and guided him into her. As his sight adjusted to the darkness he found himself staring down into the eyes behind the mask as if gazing into the soul of an anonymous Everywoman. Soon Eva began to moan—she was coming—and he let himself go inside her.

"Cone, let me spend the night," she breathed. "And tomorrow night. Please marry me so I can stay in America. I will take care of you, Baby. What do you say?"

He was just drunk enough, desperate enough, and eager enough to finish his book that her suggestion now seemed not so ludicrous or onerous. He sensed her breasts pressing against him and her perfume filling his head. He took in a breath, brushed damp blonde hair from her forehead, and said: "Sure, Baby. Why not?"

A cat screeched and he looked up. On the second-floor balcony of the uninhabited Hemingway House he saw a figure in dim moonlight. Then a cloud of smoke, as if the figure had puffed on a pipe. Con perceived there a shadowy man, a man who stood staring at him and shaking his head. Con blinked, and the apparition vanished.

Chapter Twenty-seven

Con and Johannsen zipped out of their wetsuits a mile from shore on the Atlantic side of the island. They'd anchored above some patch reefs that gave them four nice-sized lobsters, now crawling among their dive fins, gloves, and snorkel masks on Tailchaser's stern. The water had cooled to seventy-five degrees, meaning no more risk of hurricanes. That day the Atlantic lay flat and clear; the December sky radiated royal blue.

Johannsen grabbed two beers from the cooler and they lounged on the padded benches forward, warming in the sun.

"Women are trouble," said Con, staring out across the open sea. "You always get more than you bargained for."

"Saw the notice in *The Citizen*."

"Who'd think she'd buy a wedding announcement? She's practically a hooker."

"Someone posted it at the tennis courts."

Con glared at him. "You bastard."

The beer came bitter and cold, washing the salty taste from Con's mouth. He turned away and gazed at the monotonous blue of sea and sky. "Thought it would be a five-minute thing at the courthouse. Not a Christmas Eve extravaganza at Fort Zach."

"Good documentation for her Immigration file."

"The whole marriage thing's giving me the willies."

"What's better, Martens: correcting comma splices in Texas or taking a two-year honeymoon with a Czech pro in Key West?"

"Whoring is whoring."

"Money is money."

"Ignoble and damaging for an artist to have to worry about it."

"You could live under the mangroves and eat the catch-of-the-day. Or simply exist on the fragrance of frangipani and thus retain your purity."

"Not talking about abstract morality stuff but about making good writing and how prostituting yourself harms it."

"Maybe you can get an advance. How's it going?"

Con shook his head and took another swallow of beer. "Best not to talk about it or let anyone else see it, including the agent. Hemingway said you can bitch your material and make it concrete when it should be malleable."

"What did he say about marrying for money? He had a suspicious habit of falling for heiresses."

"Thanks for pointing out that I'm a cut-rate whore."

"To the contrary: The wedding will make you an honest man."

Con shook his head. "Guess I should have a best man."

Johannsen got up to piss over the side. "Happy to."

"And while you're up, get me another beer. I may stay drunk till Christmas."

"Why quit then?"

*

Con stood on his verandah nibbling a Santa-shaped

sugar-cookie and watching the aluminum Christmas tree planted on the front porch across the street turning endlessly on its motorized pedestal. The little old lady who lived there also had electronic Christmas music playing from a loudspeaker at the tree's base—"O, Little Town of Bethlehem," currently.

The previous week, when he lay in his hammock on the verandah trying to write and she had the music going, he couldn't get anything done. So he marched over, knocked on her door, and asked her to turn it off. But he felt like hell afterward, remembering the hurt face she'd pulled. So, since it was now Christmas Eve, he went over to apologize and asked her to crank up the music. Which she did, along with forcing Christmas cookies on him.

He heard a low growl coming up the street and saw Johannsen pull to the curb below in his Porsche. He came up the stairs and onto the verandah with a bottle of Dom Pérignon and two fluted glasses. "Merry Christmas!"

"Right."

Johannsen looked him up and down. "I sense something different about you."

"My ashen complexion?"

"Never seen you in long pants."

Con hooked his thumbs in his belt and turned to model his cream-colored slacks.

"Eva bought them for me. And the matching silk guayabera."

"She has good taste in clothes if not men. She could have had me."

Con watched as Johannsen uncorked and poured the champagne. "I keep thinking something will happen so I won't have to marry her. I've even been buying lottery tickets and playing the Pick Six at Calder."

They touched glasses and drank.

Johannsen said: "Still a half hour left, Martens. Time

enough for a car wreck or brain aneurysm."

"I love your gallows humor."

"There's your problem, Petruchio: You're getting married not executed."

"I've lived alone for years."

"You did okay on the cohabitation trial."

"She was on best behavior: Getting up early to fix coffee and mixing cocktails at just the right time. Not leaving her stockings hanging in the shower and never asking of my whereabouts. I.e., the usual snow job till they get their hooks in you."

"Snow job, blow job. She's a beautiful young woman who's devoted to you and will help support you so you can finish your book. In return you're saving her from the ruins of communism. Tit for tat."

"Twat for naught."

Johannsen shook his head. "Let's finish the bottle and see if your mood brightens."

Yet Con understood one source of his darkness. That night Nick had again visited him in his dreams—though this time unbidden. Again both of them plied the seas on the Pilar but at night, with Con at the helm and an obliterating fog encircling them.

"You're veering off course, Conman," Nick had said. "No! The other way. Watch those rocks! You'll sink us!"

Con had woken in a sweat, his heart thumping against his ribs.

"Fuck him."

"Beg pardon?"

Con shook his head. "Sorry. Thinking about something else."

That something being how Nick had gotten the grand house in Key West with its saltwater swimming pool out of wife number two but still managed to write good stuff, yet now nagged Con for doing similarly. But then he saw he was confusing Nick with Hemingway.

*

They rode toward Fort Zach with the top down, Con staring at the passing houses and storefronts and feeling his stomach churn.

"Balsams, fake snowflakes, and sleighs in the tropics."

"You missed Santa's arrival at Searstown on his jet-ski."

"No Christ Child on a catamaran?" Con shook his head. "Jesus save me."

Johannsen parked across from the old fort and handed a flask to Con, who sniffed it and swallowed down a dollop.

"I keep hoping for a miracle."

Johannsen took back the flask and drank. "That an intellectually able man can spend his entire life in the Land of Mammon, get a book on the bestseller list, and still not have a farthing to his name seems to me a great miracle."

"Give me the whiskey."

They walked on a shaded trail of pine needles toward the western rocks. A palm warbler twittered from a tree branch. Above the canopy of Australian pines Con saw Magnificent Frigate Birds soaring free.

"Eva wanted the wedding here because it's where I first showed her tropical fish. 'Zhey are so beautiful and free, Cone. As ve vill be. Please, Cone, marry me zhere.' How do you say 'No' to that?"

"No man should."

Ahead near the rocks where the Atlantic met the Gulf of Mexico a crowd had gathered. Con shook his head. "Look at the fucking people."

"Your ex-lovers."

As if on cue, approaching through the pines to his right Con saw a stylishly dressed blonde. "Hell."

"What?"

"Wild Cat."

"She packing?"

She spied Johannsen and Con and veered toward them, followed by a tall, gaunt, black-haired man with unshaven chin.

Johannsen asked: "Who's the guy, her hit-man?"

"I'm guessing Russian husband."

"Surprised you invited them."

"Fucking newspaper announcement."

She stopped before them on the sun-dappled path, crying and tearing at a Kleenex in her hand. Nestor, presumably, came up behind her looking Con up and down. Con thought to defend himself with, for once, the truth: He didn't know she was married. But before he could utter a word Cat said:

"Don't do it, Con. Please don't. Not for my sake. I know it's over. You'll never believe it was an accident or forgive me for lying about Nestor. But don't do what I did…" Her shoulders shook. Nestor pressed his hands to her biceps as if to offer both physical and moral support. She went on: "Don't marry to help someone else then meet the person you were meant to be with."

He looked from her to Nestor who nodded. Cat continued:

"I know you don't love me like I love you. But I love you enough to beg you not to do it, for your sake. We're forced to compromise so much in life, Con. But not this. Not your heart."

With that she broke into sobs and turned toward Nestor. He stroked her hair as she pressed her face to his chest and lifted his chin at Con.

"Please forgive us. And forgive me. She has done me a great service that saved my life. And I have done you a disservice. But it cannot be helped. Not now." Then he led her away, joining the others at the water's edge.

Johannsen held out the flask. Con took it and drank.

They moved toward the shore and setting sun, Con's eyes fixed on Eva, who stood with Nadya at her side. As he approached he saw that Eva wore low on her hips a ruffled, translucent white miniskirt. A white tank top showed her bronzed midriff and gold navel-ring. Her blonde hair was braided atop her head and festooned with dainty white flowers. When she saw him, she smiled.

What the hell, Con thought, and smiled back. Life was a miracle, a miraculous flowing stream of myriad creatures. Might as well jump in. He took her hand, turned toward the crowd, and felt his heart thump.

In front he spied Sandra with a short, prosperous-looking man: her agent, he guessed. Next to her stood Marta, glassy-eyed, though whether from vodka or tears he could not determine. Also, seemingly returned from the belly of the whale and looking years younger, Rebecca Hemingway, who gave him a wink. Off to the side, beneath a palm on the rocky shore, stood Aurora and Ricardo, the latter wearing a gold coin on a neck chain. Con's eyes then focused on Aurora, moved down her length, and saw that she was pregnant. He calculated the weeks from the night of Hurricane Hector when they made love sixteen times and came up with some four months. Time enough. He felt Johannsen's hand on his elbow.

"Steady, man."

A middle-aged woman in a turquoise pants-suit stepped forward. She carried a Bible and wore an embossed plastic nametag reading "Rev. Josephine. Fantasy Island Weddings." Her voice came to him as if from a great distance: "We are gathered here today to witness the union of Eva Tatiana Karaslova and Constantine Alexander Martens...."

Eva and Nadya smiled at him. His head spun, his stomach seemed to rise.

"Do you, Eva, take this man, Constantine..."

Even his hearing seemed to be going, as beneath the

woman's words he sensed a deep rumbling in the back of his consciousness. It grew louder and more distinct, and from the corner of his eye he saw an old fishing boat cruising up the channel from Key West Harbor. As it approached he recognized its silhouette against the setting sun: the Pilar. Behind the wheel in beige fishing shirt and cap stood Nick, broad-shouldered, dark-haired, mustached.

As Con turned back, his eyes were drawn toward Aurora by her hand moving to her throat. She fixed him with a gaze and touched the cowrie-shell necklace she wore, identical to his, as if signaling him. Compulsively he reached up to his talisman and recalled her words when she gave it to him as they swam in warm Cuban waters: "As long as your heart is pure, you will be protected."

Then, at the back of the crowd, he saw Cat silently sobbing in the arms of her husband, who stared at him meaningfully.

"And do you, Constantine, take Eva to be your lawfully wedded wife, to have and to hold from this day forward, for better or for worse, for richer, for poorer, in sickness and in health, to love and to cherish, till death do us part?"

He looked to Eva, mind racing: Till Green Card do us part. Swearing a spurious oath before God and Man, the former likely indifferent if extant or merely a non-participant observer or maybe even dead. If He were looking out for me, Con reasoned, He'd give me my daily bread and I wouldn't be in this fix marrying for money and using His name so flippantly and still hoping for a miracle. Cat's admonition not to compromise his heart also reprised in his consciousness. The Pilar quieted as Nick cut the motor. All was dead still now except for the waves slapping at the rocks as a Magnificent Frigate Bird circled silently above.

Everyone stared at him: Sandra, Marta, and Rebecca; Cat and Nestor; Ricardo and Aurora; Josephine and Johannsen; Nadya, and Eva. Even Nick had fixed his gaze on

Con from the stern of the Pilar, and Con recalled his last advice, about submitting to the gods he was serving and remembering what he was there for. Nick lifted a hand and called, but his words were lost in the sound of the surf. Logically he might have been wishing him good luck, but Con thought otherwise, thought he could read his lips, or his mind: "Permission granted to come aboard."

Con turned back to Eva, stared into her eyes, and said: "I...do svidaniye!"

He grabbed her shoulders and pressed a kiss on her lips. Then he took two quick steps over the rocks, leapt into the blue-green sea headfirst, and started kicking toward the Pilar. From the shore behind him he heard gasps, hoots, and a smattering of applause. A rock zipped past his head and splashed in the water before him, then another. He wedged off his sandals and dove deeper into the cool, clear sea.

Among the rocks he spied multicolored parrotfish and elegant angelfish, black-striped sergeant majors and glittering blue tang. Here's some material for you, he told himself: escaping by the skin of your teeth, reborn in salty waters, off to God-knows-where. But in the right direction: toward your heart's desires, not the ginned-up ones you find on shore. He swam for the Pilar, his *deus ex machina*. And who knows, he thought, maybe Nick was a god or an angel waiting to extract him from his predicament.

Looking up, he saw the boat's crusty bottom and stroked toward it. Nick had dropped the ladder. When Con stepped on the bottom rung Nick extended a thick hand toward him. He grasped it, and off they went, out into the Gulf Stream.

PART FOUR: RETURN

Chapter Twenty-eight

A warm May morning. Con steered the Pilar up the channel past the Stock Island power plant starboard and, portside, a rusting freighter that floated disused. Across from the shrimp docks where lobster boats bobbed now that the season had ended, Nick lifted his chin toward open cleats beyond an old 30-foot sloop. Con headed the boat there, eased it up to the bumpers, and cut the engine. A weathered, stringy man in shorts, can of beer in hand, appeared from inside the shed and threw him a line.

Nick led Con down the dock, up a gangway, and past fishing boats, live-aboards, and small shrimpers moored there, the smell of gasoline and decaying fish hanging in the still air. The solid earth beneath Con's feet felt odd now. After months on the water, he'd got his sea legs under him and found it awkward to walk on flat, steady terrain.

But his walk felt uncertain for another reason. He had always associated sex only with pleasure, never with pro-creation. But now he would face Aurora and his child. And although she had promised that her fate would not be his concern if he helped her across, this was different. The fate of the child was also involved.

At a weathered pre-fab houseboat with potted palms both fore and aft, Nick stopped and called: "¡Hola! ¿Estás a casa?"

In an open doorway Ricardo appeared in a blue Speedo and flip-flops. They stepped aboard to shake hands. "I get your letters," he said in English. "All is well....Sientense."

They followed him aft and sat on folding aluminum lawn chairs under a beach umbrella bungeed to the rail. Ricardo disappeared inside and soon returned with three bottles of Hatuey lager. They knocked them together.

"¡Bienvenidos! Welcome home."

"Gracias...¿Y Aurora?" asked Nick. "It goes well with her and her child?"

"Sí. Both she and Constantino are good."

Con took a swallow of beer and sounded the child's name in his head. He felt lightheaded, torn between pride and trepidation.

"¡Mira!" said Ricardo. "Here she comes."

Con turned and licked dry lips. Aurora had stepped from the cabin in jeans and tee-shirt. In her arms she carried an infant wrapped in a white crib-blanket. Nick stood and Con followed. She planted a kiss on Nick's cheek then Con's, and a vanilla aroma wafted up to him from the child. He looked down to Constantino, started, and stared, transfixed. For the child was ebony, with a head of tight-curled black hair and chocolate eyes. When Con looked up to Aurora, she smiled at him and said blandly: "Su padre queda en Habana...His father remains in Havana. But soon I hope he too will find a way here."

"Espero."

She handed the child to Con, saying, "We have named him after you, for it was you who allowed him to be born here."

Con held the child as he might an overloaded grocery

sack, fearful of spilling its contents. Soon he passed him to Nick, who cradled the infant easily in his arm and cooed to him. Together Aurora and Con stepped toward the bow, where a trio of fishing rods leaned against the rail. She looked down into the slick, greenish water.

"Lo siento, Constantino. I was not honest with you. This was why I had to come here and had you help me. So my child would be born an American citizen."

"Then you were pregnant when we met?"

She nodded. "I found out just that day, the day you and Señor Adams came to the Casa de Tango. I couldn't tell Ricardo for fear he would not leave if he knew I was embarazada, that he would stay to care for me and end up in prison."

She pressed her hands together as if in prayer and went on: "Then, when you returned that morning and we drove to the beach and talked about America, I could not help myself. I would have done anything to come. Can you forgive me?"

Con looked into her eyes, which darted beseechingly from side to side. He let out a breath. "Claro. Yo entiendo. It is nothing. I am happy that you and your child are well and hope his father can join his family soon. I was afraid, when I saw you pregnant at the wedding ceremony…"

She frowned. "Afraid?"

"That it was my child."

Her frown deepened as a passing cloud placed her face in shadow. "How could that be?"

He leaned away from her. "Well, from the night of the hurricane."

"But we would have had to make love."

He studied her to see if she was pulling his leg. But she continued to stare at him dubiously, even as the cloud moved on, lighting Aurora's unfathomable blue eyes with sun.

*

Aurora made lunch, which Con ate warily. He did not trust her—not what she cooked nor what she claimed. But he mistrusted his own perceptions as well. He didn't know what to believe anymore. Anything seemed possible: reincarnated writers, hallucinogenic chicken, and dream sex that was better than the real thing.

As they ate shrimp and rice, Nick filled in Ricardo on what they had learned over the winter: conditions at the wreck sites they scouted, what equipment and crew they'd need, how they'd provision their treasure-hunting expedition. Meanwhile Con told Aurora about the outlying Cuban islands where they had put in, the string of Bahamian keys they had lolled at, and all they had seen—the people, the birds, the fish, the sea.

And she told him her news: She'd gotten a gig singing at the Casa Marina piano bar, which came about after Johannsen took her to karaoke night at the Garrison Bight marina, where she wowed the crowd singing old Cuban songs.

After lunch, as Nick and Ricardo continued to talk business, Con returned to the Pilar and ran the boat back out on the Atlantic. Then he cut across to the Gulf under the Boca Chica Bridge, slid up Key Haven to the portside, and took the boat into the canal where Johannsen's house sat. He putted past fine homes with mature palms, tennis courts, and shiny sport-fishing boats moored at their docks. The hot sun hung lowering ahead and slightly to starboard.

When he got to Johannsen's place he spied Tailchaser tied at the dock and cut the engine to glide up behind her. As he did, he noticed two topless, bikini-clad women atop chaise longues on the brick patio there—a redhead lying on her back and a blonde facedown. When the redhead rose on her elbows to gaze at him and the Pilar, he recognized Nadya. Then the bronzed blonde turned to her side and stared at him through oversized sunglasses, and he saw it was Eva. When she realized it was Con, she covered her breasts with her hands—an odd piece of modesty at this point, he thought—and found her bikini top on the bricks.

He secured the Pilar at the concrete dock and stepped ashore to the fragrance of coconut tanning oil. Moving toward the Czech, he said: "Eva, I'm sorry. I had to follow my heart."

She rose, came to him, and raised her hand as if to slap him. He stood with arms at his sides, ready to take it. However, she only patted his cheek and shook a finger at him. "You are a very bad boy, Cone. Leaving poor Eva for Immigration police and deportation. But I forgive you. It is your loss."

A voice came from above: "And my gain."

He looked up to see Johannsen descending the circular metal stairs, a Heineken twelve-pack in hand. Jojo crossed the patio and handed Con a beer by way of greeting, then gave one to each woman. Next he stepped aboard Tailchaser with the remaining bottles.

"Come on, Con. I need to spear dinner."

*

At the end of the canal Johannsen throttled up, headed Tailchaser out into the Gulf, and opened a beer. He hollered over the engine noise: "Found some nice patch reefs about a mile out. Lots of yellowtail and grouper."

Ten minutes later, following the guide of his GPS, he throttled down, dropped anchor, and went over the side with snorkel mask and spear gun.

Con stayed on board, stretched aft under the bimini, sipping a beer. Over the winter his skin had grown darker, his hair even blonder from the sun. He lay on the padded bench staring at puffy clouds above, feeling the benign sea gently rocking him and hearing its intermittent slap against the hull. Twice Johannsen swam back to the boat with snappers he'd speared then finally came up the ladder with an impaled black grouper.

"I'm getting good at this."

"Might be the target practice you get at home."

Johannsen pried a cap off a green bottle and lifted it to Con: "Na zdrovye!"

"¡Salud!"

"Let me tell you what happened…" Johannsen said, lowering himself into the captain's chair.

Con lifted himself on his elbow to listen.

"After you left Eva at the altar, Marta wrote a story about it—'Groom Takes the Plunge'—that made *The Citizen*'s front page and inadvertently drew official attention to Eva's illegal status. Immigration came looking for her at home while she was at work and arrested her two roommates, whom they shipped back to Russia. She went into hiding on Stock Island with Nadya, who prevailed on me to help. So I cut myself a deal." Johannsen took a long drink from his bottle. "Eva became the second Mrs. Joseph Johannsen until she gets her Green Card, and the three of us have formed a damn interesting ad hoc family."

"Nice work."

"But there was one crucial condition for Eva: She had to forgive you. No way she comes between us."

"Thanks. Never thought the feds would come after her. I wasn't thinking."

"Just as well. Not your strong suit."

"Glad you were able to step in."

"Marta felt like hell when she saw what she'd unleashed."

"I'll have to look her up."

"You'll have to look in Miami. Got her drinking under control and took a job at the *Herald* covering Cuba."

"Another successful escape."

"And what of yours? Clean?"

Con knew he was alluding to Aurora's pregnancy, and so told him how she had manipulated him to come across and of the father trapped in Havana. He also recounted how he had passed the last few months:

"Nick and I hung around the Dry Tortugas, mostly. Caught lots of fish. Drank beer with Cuban lobstermen. Did some diving and snorkeling scouting wreck sites. Read and wrote in longhand. I never showed Nick my manuscript and never talked about it specifically. But when I was stuck or headed off compass he'd get me back on course, steering me inside myself and to the things I knew were true."

Con looked off at the setting sun.

"You're smiling," said Johannsen.

"Was I?"

"For the past half hour."

"Thinking about what Nick said, about how hard writing is but how nothing makes you feel better. How you suffer like a bastard when you don't write and feel great when you do, and how you feel empty and fucked out after."

"Eloquently put."

Con got himself another beer and went on: "We rode out the winter that way though our winter came warm and flat. Cruised over to the Bahamas and Bimini then down to some of the smaller Cuban islands, avoiding civilization as best we could."

"Sounds like a dream. But..."

Con saw the question on Johannsen's face but it was one he couldn't answer.

"If you're wondering about Nick, so am I. Let's put it this way: Either he's benignly insane or the best damn actor in the world. Or maybe..."

"No, Con, don't say it. Next you'll be telling me you believe in Santa Claus."

Con sucked on his beer and looked at the dimming sun sinking beyond Woman Key. "You remember how easy it was as a child to embrace Santa, the tooth fairy, and leprechauns? When giants lived in the clouds and bears could talk and miracles happened? How we innocently accepted all that to explain things beyond our ken, which made the world seem enchanted? Maybe the world is still enchanted but we've become too calloused and sophisticated to notice. Maybe angels still exist and maybe miracles still happen. I don't want to rule them out. Sometimes fantastic explanations come closer to the truth."

Johannsen pursed his lips and nodded slowly. Finally he asked: "Did you finish the novel?"

Con shrugged. "As much a memoir as it is a novel. Fact, fiction…My life's become so surreal that half the time I don't know whether I'm dreaming or awake."

"I know what you mean. Every morning when I wake in the middle of the Soviet bloc I have to pinch myself. But…" A cottony cloud passed before the dropping sun and with it came a cooling breeze. Johannsen bit his lip as if riding a wave of emotion. "You know, Eva's not as tough as she makes out to be. At heart she's quite a soft and vulnerable creature."

Con chugged down some Heineken. "You figure this out all on your own?"

"I'm a mental giant, not an intuitive genius like you. Takes me longer to see the obvious qualities in people."

"Sounds like you're falling in love."

"She is my wife."

"What about Nadya?"

"Exiled to Siberia, that is, the guest room, for re-education."

"Carry on, commissar."

"What about you? Need money?"

"Thanks, I might. Nick gave me some cash for helping

him scout treasure sites but it won't last long. Have to find work."

"You? Work?"

"It's okay. Everything's okay now that I'm writing again…I had it all wrong, worrying about money and chasing after it and hurting Eva and others in the process. I should have listened to the Buddha on that score. I didn't need money. I needed to become myself again. To embrace the gods I'd abandoned. Once I did that everything fell into place."

"How about a place to stay?"

"I'm looking."

"What about your old digs?"

"I called Berman from the Bahamas last week. Said he'd rented it to some lawyer."

"The only ones who can afford Old Town these days."

"I'll just stay on the Pilar and shower at the shrimp docks until I can find a job and a cheap place to live."

Johannsen shook his head. "Sounds like hell: no AC, TV, wine cellar or women."

Con swallowed down his beer. "I have to tell you something miraculous, Jojo, something you won't believe: I wouldn't trade places with you."

Johannsen laughed as he reached for another beer. "Writers!"

Chapter Twenty-nine

Next morning, Saturday, Con went by his old place on Elizabeth Street to collect his bicycle, which still sat chained inside the fence, and his clothes. After he had taken his Christmas Eve leap he wrote to tell Berman, who had his meager possessions boxed and stowed somewhere in the apartment. Con knocked but got no response. He turned away feeling odd about knocking on his own door.

He biked around Old Town. Nothing had changed. Chickens, which tourists found so quaint, still crowing raucously; out-of-towners driving the wrong way down one-way streets; folks drinking breakfast at sidewalk cafes. But the town lay relatively quiet, the tourist season having passed. Which meant fewer opportunities to find writing students, and got him thinking about his former clients. He ended up at the Conch house where Rebecca Hemingway lived, though he wondered if she was still alive. However, he recalled that the last time he saw her, at his aborted wedding ceremony, she had appeared uncharacteristically healthy and happy.

Inside the white picket fence he chained his Trek to

a silver palm and mounted the back stairs. At the top he heard symphonic music coming through the screen door. He knocked and called her name.

Rebecca appeared at the door wearing an apron over jogging clothes. She pushed the door open, wooden spoon in hand, to hug him. "You're alive and well."

"You too."

She pulled him inside. "Thanks to you."

He sat at the breakfast counter sipping coffee while she assembled a fish stew. He lifted his chin toward the steaming Dutch oven atop the range.

"Dinner party tonight?"

"Small one. Met a man."

"Not again."

"This is different. We're having such fun."

"Fun? Is this the Rebecca Hemingway I know?"

She turned from the range. "She's gone. Dead and gone. I killed her off," she said reaching for a butcher knife, "as promised."

Chopping an onion in front of him, she went on: "Did as you suggested: contacted a social worker, who found me some help. They got it early enough, it seems. I won't be able to have children but I figure I'm child enough for any man." She wiped tears from her eyes with the back of her hand. "Damn onions...You gave me the proper kick in the ass at the right time. You were right: You never know if something good is just around the corner."

"Where'd you meet him?"

"Key West High."

"Upperclassman?"

She scraped the onions from the cutting board into the pot and the aroma came to him. "Another English teacher."

"'Another'?"

"Started in January."

"As penance for your previous dissolute life?"

She smiled. "It's not so bad. Most are good kids, and they certainly need the help."

"What about your book?"

She wiped her hands on her apron. "I've given up writing. Dumped introspection and stopped beating up on myself. Trying to accept things as they are, myself included. Can't tell you how much happier I am focusing on helping my students and pleasing Alan."

"Sounds healthy."

"You should try it."

"Quit writing?"

"Teaching. We need English teachers. You could substitute for the rest of the semester and start fulltime in August."

"That word 'fulltime' gives me chills."

"Then just sub for now and see how you like it. I assume you need money."

"Nice to have some touchstones. Guess I'd need some clothes: long pants, shoes, a shirt. Though I do still have my wedding outfit on board."

"I didn't like you much for that: jilting Eva."

He looked at his black coffee. "I didn't think much of it either. Damn rotten thing to do to her, going back on my word. But I wasn't in control. Other forces intervened."

Rebecca looked at him and blinked. "You're not getting religion are you?"

Con shook his head. "Not so you'd notice. But…Let's put it this way: Lots of spooky occurrences recently for which I have no explanation."

"Now you're scaring me."

"Not so scary. Beneficent spooks."

They chatted more about teaching, and he summarized the previous five months for her: his sojourn with Nick, his return, Eva's marriage, Marta's relocation, everything except his work on his book, which, following Nick's advice, he still kept close to the vest.

He left feeling happy for Rebecca, who seemed to have rescued herself and settled into a benignly mundane life, but a bit melancholy about his own, for some reason. As he pedaled up to Stock Island and the Pilar, Con felt ill at ease, though he had no idea why—as if a fog had gathered on the edges of his consciousness. Yeah, it was great to be writing again. That meant everything, he told himself. Still...

Of course it would be nice to be normal, at least in some ways—not to suffer, as Rebecca had, under the constant introspection and concern about your work. Nice not to have to worry so damn much about yourself. But that was part of it, he knew. Obsessions came at a cost.

*

When Con arrived at the Pilar he found Nick on deck reading *Anna Karenina*. Con went to the ice chest and pulled out a beer. "You?"

Nick nodded. "Reading and writing both make me thirsty."

Con levered the caps off two bottles and handed one to Nick, thinking how Tolstoy began *Anna*: "Happy families are all alike; every unhappy family is unhappy in its own way."

"And what about happy?"

Nick put down his book. "When you are writing and do it right you get a great happiness. But whenever I stopped writing for a month or two and went on a trip I felt absolutely animally happy. They are very different, Conman, but one is as important as the other when you realize how short life is."

Con drank and nodded. "I guess so."

"Then after the writing and the trip there is the happiness of the homecoming."

As Nick said it, the bothersome fog lifted for Con and

he saw the source of his melancholy: Hemingway had had Paris, the house in Key West, the Finca Vijia in Cuba, and, finally, the home in Ketchum, Idaho. And when he, Con, knocked that morning at the door of his home—the only home he had known for years—no one had let him in.

Chapter Thirty

Sunday morning he loaded his tennis racquet and snorkel gear in his backpack and biked to Bayview Park for doubles then, at noon, over to the beach at Fort Zach. There he lay in the shade of the pines reading the newspaper and later snorkeled out beyond the rocks. Thanks to light northerly winds, the water lay clear and welcoming. On the bottom in some fifteen feet of sea he spied a starfish. A good omen, he thought, and he made a wish on it: that he would somehow find himself a home.

Rebecca's suggestion about substitute teaching at Key West High kept returning to consciousness throughout the day. Perhaps a relatively painless stopgap while he finished his book and found new writing students. So on his way back up island to the Pilar, he swung by his old place on Elizabeth Street, hoping to find someone home and collect his clothes. When he braked to a stop on the sidewalk he saw that the downstairs door stood open. He dismounted, dropped his backpack on the porch, and knocked on the screen door. After a minute he knocked again and called: "Anyone home?"

Finally, as he remounted his bike and was about to pedal off, he heard footsteps on the stairs. A pair of shapely legs appeared. Pushing through the screen door, Cat stepped willowy onto the porch in cut-offs and tank top. She looked at him and let out a breath as if after a great exertion. "You finally found me."

"That's funny," Con said, heart pounding. "Wasn't even looking for you."

"Sure you were. You just didn't know it."

A breeze off the Gulf rattled the traveler palm behind him then quieted.

"Actually, I was looking for my clothes and computer. What are you doing here?"

"I live here."

"Since when?"

"Since Nestor and I divorced."

Con looked her up and down searching for words, trying to figure where the traps lay, and whether or not he wanted to stumble into them.

"Congratulations in order, I guess."

She moved across the porch to the balustrade and the scent of patchouli came with her. Her pale blue eyes darted from side to side taking him in; her chest heaved as if with emotion. "Oh, Con…"

He found himself squeezing the bike's handlebars and relaxed his grip. "What about your job?"

"Ditched that as well. Set up an immigration practice here. Your former fiancée was my first client. I managed to stall her deportation until she found a man who wasn't so skittish."

"Bullets and banns always make me jumpy."

"I threw that darn gun off the Boca Chica Bridge."

"That's comforting."

"That's all I want to be to you, Con: a comfort. Not a problem, not a burden, not a wife or chaperone."

"What about executioner?"

She laid a warm hand on his forearm. "There's something we need to do."

Birds twittered in the sand tree stretching above them. He discerned competing urges: one to pedal off as fast as he could, for he felt loose and vulnerable around her, the other to embrace her.

"I'm listening," he said. "What do we need to do?"

She fixed him with a gaze. "Forgive."

"Who's forgiving whom for what?"

"Both of us, each other, for everything, past, present, future."

Here, he sensed, lay one of those traps. But he moved ahead anyway. "Why?"

"So we can be together. So we can love each other without ire or angst or jealousy."

"Sounds more like benign indifference—my usual choice. Anyway, love's overrated."

"Not if you do it right. And I thought we did it pretty well."

Although he sat in the shade and another breeze again rustled the palm fronds, he felt hot, his hands perspiring.

"I'm still wary of Wild Cat."

"She's Pussy Cat now, and purring. Now that she's changed the things that made her beastly."

Con studied her. "I don't know."

"Take your time. I'm not going anywhere. Get to know me again without all the baggage I had before…" An ambulance roared up Fleming Street, siren screaming. When the air hung quiet again, she went on: "I don't want to hurt or hinder you. I just want to be a helpmate."

He folded his arms across his chest and noticed beads of perspiration above her lip. "Well, Pussy Cat, you can help me by finding my clothes. Berman said he stowed them away upstairs."

She pursed her lips, nodding. "Good. That's a start. Lock up your bike," she said, turning and retreating through the screen door. But then she paused as if she had an idea and glanced back over her shoulder. "First we better look under the bed."

Epilogue

The sun had set by the time Con got home from tennis, yet the sky had not darkened. Wispy clouds flamed out over the island from the west—fire orange and gold against cobalt, the sort of improbable sky that, in an amateur painting, made you smile.

He found Cat on the verandah, sitting at the table, red-eyed, tears drying on her gaunt cheeks.

"What's wrong, Baby?"

She bit her lip and shook her head. He sat across from her and lay his hand open on the tablecloth. She kept her hands in her lap.

"I broke my promise." She sniffled and wiped her eyes with the back of her hand.

"What promise?"

"To never again be jealous."

When he frowned, she raised her hands from her lap. In them she held the manuscript he had given her to read. He had waited until the novel was as good as he could get it. He wrote and rewrote—he couldn't count the times he had studied each sentence, each word and deed of every character, the movement and pace of the narrative; how many times he had gone through to layer in, stratum by stratum, the sensory details that put the reader there—in Key West, in Cuba, on the sea—the concrete things that conveyed the emotion. Then he had abandoned it for months and came back to it with fresh eyes and a clear mind, to avoid having his judgment impaired by infatuation with it. More months of getting it right, compressing, strengthening, enriching; and cutting, cutting, cutting. Then, when it was done, when he was sure it was done and it was good, as good as anything he had ever done, with the verve and solemnity of his early short stories, with the accumulated craft and wisdom he had gained over decades of listening, reading, and writing, and striving to do it right, he gave it to her to read.

"It's beautiful, Con. I feel as if I've lived it."

"Thank you. That's the greatest praise."

"There's grace and great heart. It's solid and serious. But I am so jealous."

"I had help," he said, touching the rabbit's foot he carried in his pocket.

She shook her head. "Not jealous of your gift. It's that I now know this is your first love."

He reached up and took her hand, warm and moist. He felt her pulse beat.

"No, nothing makes me feel better. I wrote it for me but I wrote it for you too, Cat. That was in my mind, always. First, I wrote for me, then for you."

She took a breath that made her shoulders rise. She wiped her eyes once again, stood, and touched his shoulder. "I'll bet you need a beer." She moved inside and as she retreated called out the open doorway: "There's a letter for you."

He went to his desk in the hallway. There positioned on his laptop he found an envelope with a colorful parrot pictured on the stamp. He read the Nassau postmark, recognized Nick's handwriting, and tore it open.

Nick acknowledged getting Con's letter at Nassau General Delivery and congratulated him on his reconciliation with Cat and his discipline with his book, but with this caution:

…Ultimately, Conman, the publishing and books et cetera and what people say about your work don't matter a damn. Publicity, admiration, adulation, or simply being fashionable are all worthless. The only real reward is that which is within ourselves. We can write and leave a legacy for a while but maybe it's just ego and ink that will someday disappear. Finding sunken treasure don't matter either. At least not the literal kind though the hunt for it is most always good. What does matter is being true to yourself and your calling and you've done that. But if your book is good it is about something you know and is truly written and reading it over you see that this is so. So let the boys yip, and the noise will have the pleasant sound coyotes make on a cold night when they are out in the snow and you are in your own cabin that you have built or paid for with your work.

Con felt a hand on his shoulder, turned, and took a sweating bottle of lager from Cat. He kissed her fingertips and bent again to the letter as she moved away.

But I also see that for all your attempts to sit alone and write you keep bumping into those around you and affecting them in some helpful way, as if an unconscious catalyst for good. All your women—Eva, Aurora, Rebecca, Marta, Sandra, and Wild Cat—have landed on their feet as have Johannsen, Ricardo, Constantino, and myself, thanks in part to your interference, stumbling variety. And if that's all there is, infecting folks with good luck and good cheer—along with appreciating the sunsets, seas, women, and wine—I'd take it.

But it goes both ways. You've profited by others' presence in your life, as you acknowledged in your stated "capitulation" to Cat, who's helped get you back in the swim. Sometimes you just have to leap into the current and see where it takes you, entrusting yourself to Providence. None of us can do it alone no matter what we need to do. I always took all the help I could get—from Ezra, Gertrude, Sherwood and the rest, living and dead or otherwise.

Speaking of which, don't worry yourself too much on how I got to where I am or where I came from. Or about nailing down what actually transpired between you and Aurora or any of it. It don't make no difference what's real and what's not, what actually happened or what you imagined, long as you know what's true. And we know this much is true: The world's a swell place to see and visit but even more beautiful to feel. That's why we write and why we live. So be bold and know that miracles happen. We each have our own story and the job is to live it well with courage, discipline, faith, and humility, to be the heroes of our own lives or die trying.

Your correspondent,
Nick Adams

Con folded the letter away and pushed himself up from the desk. He guessed that would be the last he'd hear from Nick for awhile and perhaps forever.

But he knew that Nick's words—both those he spoke to him and those he claimed to have written—would stay with him always. And he figured that if he ever needed him again he'd show up at just the right time.

* * *

Acknowledgements

My sincere thanks to the Cuban expatriates and their loved ones who generously recounted for me their flight from their homeland. And to all the friends, acquaintances, patrons and mentors who have helped shape and enrich my Key West experience over the years and thus contributed to this book. Those include Leslie M., Jana K., Guillermo B., Charlie W., Richard B., Bienvenidos D., Jayne N., Aurelia S., Zdenic R., Tori M., Joe E., Ellen P., Joel B., John L., Pamela L., Carter D., Greer N., John H., Harvey W., Tom B., David S., Rodger D., Mary O., Steve P., Robert A., Tom R., Terry M., Rosalind B., Sid G., Elizabeth S., and Ernest H.

* * *